FEATHER OF PROPHECY

MERGED SERIES
BOOK 4

CLAUDIA BLOOD

DRAGON BANE PUBLISHING

1

WREN

Pride and excitement made Wren fluff his feathers. His father trusted him to protect himself and his sister on a trip to the West Market. He'd never been given this responsibility or freedom. He'd never been allowed to venture down from their mountain home into New Nadezhda by himself, and being able to take Alesia, his cosseted twin, conferred a high honor.

"Look!" Alesia danced on her toes but managed to keep her cloak tucked around her. She pointed to a building on the corner. The bright light sparkled on the dew on the cobblestones, making everything seem new. The smell of honeyed cookies wafted to Wren from the open door.

He smiled at his sister. "Let's get one."

They entered the shop and the bell jangled. A human used a long wooden paddle to pull the breakfast treats out of the oven.

The smell of baked bread and honey with cinnamon filled the room.

"Oh, can we have one?" Alesia whispered and gripped his arm.

He patted her hand and said to the baker, "May we have two, please?"

The man turned with a soft whirr and metal ping and smiled. "Of course, Prince." Wren recognized him as someone his father had aided. The whir and the ping were sounds from the clever mechanism on the man's left foot that helped him walk. The Aero's artisans had built the device on his father's orders.

The human took the two honey cakes and placed them in the eating pouch and handed them to Wren.

Wren fished out a few coins and put them on the counter. "Thank you."

"No charge." The man crossed his arms.

"Please, take the money." Alesia's voice was soft and full of entreaty.

The man stared at her for a moment and then loosened his arms and nodded. "Yes, Princess."

Wren would not have been able to resist her request and was not surprised that the human had been unable to as well. Something about his sister made people want to aid her.

Wren and Alesia left, each holding a wrapped cake. The honey tasted like sunshine and reminded him of an early morning song.

"Can we try that?" Alesia was already done with her treat. She pointed to a shop labeled "Fortune Teller."

Wren shivered. His family already had a curse and a prophecy handed down in the royal family. *Two halves united shall burn and be reborn.*

The last thing he or his family needed was another prophecy. No one knew what the first one meant. The fact that two members of his family had died by fire just added to his unease.

The fortune teller shop was different from the others on the street, exuding a sense of foreboding. He had not been to the city often, and Wren had never noticed the shop before.

He glanced at his sister to say no but saw her excitement clearly written on her face. Her wide smile and sparkling eyes begged him to say yes. He hesitated. Keeping his sister safe was the most important thing to him. A close second was her happiness.

She was just as adept at reading Wren's expression because she said, "Oh, come on, Wren, how much danger can we be in? Dad sent someone to watch over us." She waved her hand at the nearby roof.

One of his father's guards sat on the roof watching them. How had Wren missed the sun glinting off that much armor?

The feeling of independence and trust disappeared. Frustration and anger roiled in his gut. He clenched his teeth 'til they ached. Instead of telling her no, which was probably the right thing, he took her hand and led her to the shop.

The door opened with a groan that sent a shiver down his spine. He'd taken enough of his apprentice training to feel the press of magic in the shop. The small entry opened into a large room. Most of the magic emanated from something covered in the middle of the wooden table in the far corner. Drapes hung not only on the windows making the interior dim, but nearby that looked like they could be closed for privacy.

The aura didn't seem to be malicious, at least not yet. But he got the impression that the magic watched him and his sister. He didn't like the feel of its gaze upon her, so he turned to go.

"Welcome to Madam Red's shop." The voice came from a dark corner on his left side.

A woman stepped from the shadows. She looked like a human, but something about her aura said she was anything but. Curly, auburn hair spilled across her shoulder and blended into scarlet, layered silk. The different red colors in her garb gave the illusion that flames hovered around her.

Wren backed his sister toward the door.

"I am not here to harm you. I can clearly see your futures," the woman said softly.

"I want to know," Alesia sang out and pushed forward. Her face was bright and excited.

The kind smile that the woman gave Alesia convinced him to stay. Divination magic was not the easiest to control. If a person was good at it, they could give a hint to the future. If they were bad at that type of magic or unlucky, they might as well make up the future for how accurate the fortune would be.

"Are you Madam Red?" Wren glanced around the dim interior and then focused on the woman.

"I am, young prince." The woman gave him a polite smile. "Come sit here." She led them to a small round table in the corner. She pulled out a chair and gestured to Alesia to sit. When Alesia did, Madam Red invited Wren to sit too.

He moved to the table and sat at the edge of the chair.

Madam Red removed a cloth from a fist-sized, clear crystal. The light sparkled on the gem's surface. Under the surface, white and red clouds rolled past.

The magic strengthened and the otherness and power puffed the feathers between his shoulders. He glanced at his sister to see if she could feel the power.

She sat frozen and stared into the gem, her blue eyes wide and her goofy and excited smile beaming from her lips. This was the smile she had used when they had found a mine cart and decided to take it through the mountain. Luckily when the ride ended with them launching off the rails and into the cavern, their wings had saved them.

Madam Red cleared her throat. She had sat at the table across from them while he was distracted.

"What's wrong with my sister?" Wren froze as Madam Red's eyes shifted from brown to bright blue. "You are the only one who can right this wrong and save her."

Wren's throat suddenly went dry. This was a test. There were always tests. He swallowed and pushed down his fear. "What must I do?"

She smiled. "There is a prophecy for you. And a word of advice."

Wren nodded. He knew he would have to memorize the words as they would never be repeated. As soon as he could, he would have to write the words down so the prediction could be put in the chronicle.

Her gaze lifted to the ceiling. She shivered and her silk garb flickered around her like flames.

> Son and daughter of the saviors of fenix
> Time runs out to repair
> that which was sundered after the Merge
> Isolate the pair until first light on her day of birth
> Seek the kept flame and release
> Two halves united shall burn and be reborn
> Only a bound witch can save them all
> Or the immortal shall die
> and break open fully the portal to the Abyss.

Wren repeated the words in his head a few times, adding them to his memory. The middle part he'd already known. The fact that this seemed related to a prediction long held in his family sent a shiver down his spine. He'd been told about the prophecy his whole life.

Wren reviewed the parts. He'd look up fenix and see if he could find the reference. The Merge was when the human realm and his own realm came together in a sudden violent event. After three hundred years, no one was sure what had caused the Merge, only that the event had decimated populations and forced the supernatural people and humans to live together. He had no idea who the pair could be, unless that was another reference to the son and daughter mentioned. There were many ways to bind a person, but to bind a witch implied a magical connection. Nothing else in the new words made any sense. He ground his teeth but worked to relax. While frustrating, this should not affect him or his sister.

Madam Red sat motionless with her hands serenely on her lap. She gazed at Alesia, who stared back at her, and then they both turned to face Wren. Alesia's eyes were iridescent. He'd been wrong. The weight of the air shifted as if a storm approached. Whatever had possessed their grandmother and ruined her life now had a hold on his sister. He struggled to breathe with the heaviness on his chest.

"It must be done by her thirtieth birthday or all is lost."

Alesia blinked her eyes and they returned to their natural blue. The spirit finding Alesia was his fault. His throat thickened and his stomach churned.

"What is your word of advice?" Wren asked, forcing the words past the constriction.

"Run, the demons are here." The woman whirled in a circle

until the silks rose and became real fire. Heat licked out, and the flame touched his hand. Tingles consumed his hand and arm to his shoulder. He stared at the flame that surrounded his wrist. A flush of adrenaline rushed through his body. He dropped to the ground trying to put out the fire. It took him a moment to realize that he was not in any pain. His arm just tingled, and the flames receded into his skin. He took a breath to calm his wildly thumping heart.

"Wren?" Alesia's voice was sharp and snapped him out of his panic. "Madam Red is gone."

He jerked his gaze away from his arm. Alesia stared at him. Her mouth gaped open in what had to be horror.

"We have to get out of here." He shook his hand, and the tingles and the flames faded.

Wren went to the front door, but when he touched the handle, the metal burned his finger. He drew his sword and cut away the curtain that blocked the front window. A pile of burning rubble blocked the door. They were trapped in the building.

Madam Red's face appeared in the flames and formed the word "Run."

Beyond the fire, a line of women stepped into view. He couldn't see the details with the flames in the way. They linked their hands, and a sheet of black frost hit the blaze. The powerful magic wave crashed over him. Madam Red's face disappeared, and the fire rose, blocking his view. Those women must be the demons.

Run! The flames hissed at him. He jerked back. Madam Red was protecting them.

"What's wrong?" Alesia asked.

"We have to fly." Wren ran toward her and grabbed her hand. His heart thudded, and he could feel his wings open.

Alesia frowned, and her eyes narrowed. "I saw a back exit." She hurried toward the back left corner. Another multi-colored red curtain shimmered in the back. She pushed the curtain aside.

A pot bubbled on the fire in a small stone hearth. A chair with a multi-colored quilt over the back sat before the fire. The walls had no windows or doors. A small stairway led up.

He grabbed Alesia's hand and pulled her up the stairs. Perhaps the top of the house had more windows or another option for escape. The stairs opened into a large room.

A spell circle dominated the center. Candles glowed around the outside. This must be her casting chamber. Another curtain blocked the far wall, hopefully covering a window or door. He tore the curtain down to reveal a window that opened at his touch. "We have to go."

"What about Madam Red?" Alesia's high, tight voice focused him. He needed to save his sister.

"She's blocking the demons so we can escape."

The urge to see the women who were attacking the front gripped him. He could fly over. They would never see him. The itch grew stronger. He needed to know who was attacking his family. Seeing them would only take a moment. He took a step away from Alesia.

"No." Alesia's eyes transformed into iridescent swirls. She touched his arm, and heat flared under his skin. Magic tingled across his senses. The urge to see the demons faded, and he took a deep breath. Alesia had no magic of her own. The power must be from whatever possessed her.

He shivered. Grandmother could do things like this when she was possessed.

Alesia's eyes rolled up. He snatched her to his chest before she collapsed.

A sharp crack at the front of the building reminded him of

the danger they were still in. He launched through the window, opening his wings wide to support them both. He flapped hard into the air and carried his sister toward home.

He knew one thing for sure. It was his fault that the spirit had found Alesia, and he would do whatever it took to save her.

2

VALERIA

<u>Just after Dawn, Primum first, 300 years post-Merge</u>

Over fourteen years later...

"You look sad, little witch." Valeria dropped the book in her hands. The thump of the volume hitting the tiled floor had her heart racing.

Alex raised his hands as if in surrender. "I thought you had heard me." His mellow, calm voice relaxed something inside her. Alex was safe. He was so thin she could probably beat him in a fight. He had very little magic of his own. More than anything else, he was a kind soul. She was safe. Her sister was safe. The demons didn't know where either of them were.

She let out a slow breath and worked to relax her tense shoulders.

"I didn't mean to startle you." His narrow build and blond curls made him appear child-like, but he was the most learned man she'd ever met, including her new, scholarly in-laws.

She picked up the book, *Ten Ways to Exorcize a Demon*, and set the book on the shelf.

"You know I could help you find what you are looking for if you told me what was going on." Alex's voice was just as soft and kind as it had been since the first time she had come to stay.

She looked into his pale blue eyes and thought about confessing everything. Then she remembered the hatred on her grandmother's face the last time Valeria had seen her. She needed to stop calling her grandmother. Isabella was never really *her* grandmother. Not after selling the family to demons generations ago.

"I'm not sure what I can tell you to help me."

"William said you are safer if you are hidden away." Alex's voice was hesitant.

She nodded. "He thinks that having Corona and me together would make it easier for Isabella to find us." What she said was not accurate nor was that fact why she was here at the Archive.

"Because Corona is your sister?"

Another nod did not seem to be what he wanted from her. He waited, lips pursed and eyes watchful. Perhaps her brother-in-law had already informed Alex what was going on.

Valeria sighed. "What has William told you?"

"You are a witch new to her power. You have some powerful enemies who want you and your sister dead. Because of what William studies, I'm assuming that the danger is demon-related. We have had an increase in demonic activity in the city. Based on your earlier comment, Isabella poses the highest risk."

Should she tell Alex about her demonic family? With any other person the answer would be no. But this was Alex. Helpful, knowledgeable Alex who literally lived in the Archives for years. "Isabella, who I thought was my grandmother, raised me. She sold out her family line to demons a long time ago. I have no idea how long, but the women of our line are born with a demon soul and a human soul inhabiting their bodies."

"And you and your sister escaped."

"We defeated our demons to be free, but I don't know how the demons got in our line or if..." His words were not a question, but she responded anyway. Fear closed her throat. This was the real reason she had left Corona's side. Corona was pregnant and based on the family curse, if her baby was female, her baby would be born with a demon next to her human soul. The demon soul would be connected to Isabella. This connection not only would give away Corona's location but also put the child at risk of possession. "But she is pregnant..."

He gasped. "You think the family's demon curse will transfer to the new babe." He seemed to study her face. "So you are here to try and figure out how to break the curse."

Her throat clogged, and her eyes burned as she nodded. Feeling the baby move in Corona's belly had decided Valeria's next action. She would not let her niece be born with a demon soul attached to her human one. So far, Valeria had been unsuccessful at finding a way to save her niece. Corona was due within the next few weeks.

His eyes lost focus and he hummed. "Taking over a family like that must have required a great deal of power."

"Power?" She hadn't given much thought to how this had happened. To have a demon soul plucked from the Abyss and connected to a baby would be powerful magic.

"Yes, there must have been a huge influx of power to attach demons so firmly to a family." He tapped his lips and glanced away. "I need to do some research. Do you have any idea when this all happened to your ancestors?"

"She called herself grandmother, but that was not right. She always felt much older."

"So, over sixty years ago. Where did you grow up?"

"We moved a lot, but they did their ceremony on my cousin, at this two-story house surrounded by slouching buildings." She shuddered at the memory and tried not to think about how much her cousin had suffered.

At his frown, she described where the house was located and some of the nearby streets.

"That's not in this city. I wonder if you went somewhere else?" He hummed and tapped his lips in a rhythm she didn't recognize. "I am going to guess that Isabella cursed the family right after the Merge. I'm also going to guess that..." His gaze turned to her. "At this ceremony, did you actually see a demon? Not a gaseous form but actually saw one?"

Valeria thought back to that awful day when she saw her cousin go through the first blood ceremony. Her aunts hadn't looked human. They looked like black and twisted caricatures of humans. "Maybe. I was not there physically but took a spirit journey. The aunts..." She was not sure how to explain. Being in her soul form distorted the physical world. Only items and people with high personal connections appeared the same from that view.

Alex grabbed a book located next to the one she had put away and flipped through the pages. "Like this?"

He turned the book toward her. The picture sent chills down her back. Crumpled humans lay in a circle around another prone figure. Hovering above were five black shadows with red eyes. In her mind, she could see them flying around Winifred. She shuddered. "Yes, they looked like this during the first blood ceremony."

Alex nodded. "The spirit plane overlaps with where we are now and the demon world. There must be a crack that leads to the demon realm. That would allow the demon souls to attach to your family. If we closed that crack, you might break your family curse. I need to do more research, but I think—"

"Meep." The high-pitched call echoed throughout the chamber. Other voices echoed through the room with the same sound.

"Drat." Alex stiffened and glared toward the sound. "I need you to contain them while I call for help."

"Contain them? What are they?" The meeping sounds grew louder as they talked.

Alex's demeanor shifted, and a fierceness she had not expected flashed in his gaze. "Meeps swarm and set fire to everything around them." He dug through a nearby shelf and handed her a sword. "Try to keep them away from the books and artifacts."

Then before she could say anything about the futility of handing a witch a sword, Alex raced away toward the front of the Archive.

The sword glowed faintly, but unless the sword knew how to fight, the weapon would be of no use to her. She placed the sword back on the shelf and walked to where the sounds came from. She would have to rely on her own magic to defend the Archive.

Solid, warded stone made up the back of the room. How did the Meeps get in? A nervous quiver hit her stomach and her senses seemed sharper. The faint smell of vanilla came from the nearby books and, even fainter, the smell of smoldering.

The scratching sounds on stone and soft meeps seemed loudest from around the next corner. She swallowed her nerves and peeked around to assess the area. Her magic did not consist of fireballs or lightning bolts but embraced protection and enchantments. Maybe she could hold the Meeps in place until help could arrive.

The dark stone of the back wall crumbled and a fuzzy, purple, winged lizard tumbled into the room. Its nails scrabbled on the stone as the lizard flipped over. The large, purple eyes looked up at her. Then the creature sneezed and exploded in a three-foot ball of fire.

Valeria understood now why Alex was freaking out. Fire in the Archive would be devastating. The whole building and everything protected within could be lost, but this little lizard was not the malevolent creature she'd been expecting.

A dozen more meeps sounded from deeper in the hole. A hundred more sounded like they might be even deeper in the walls. Large, black, sooty patterns already spotted the tiled floor.

She let out her magical senses. The slight ringing of bells and baked bread surrounded her. The Meeps' magic didn't feel evil. They were not trying to cause damage, but they were seeking something. Something together. Strange. The next lizard's nose peeked out of the hole. The lizard sniffed and then "meeped." Yes, definitely seeking.

Running footsteps echoed behind her.

"Where's the sword? They are going to burn this place down if we can't get them contained." Alex's face reddened. "They almost took out the Archive in the neighboring town. A dozen wizards finally stopped them, but they still lost most of that building and artifacts."

She grabbed his arm before he could do something to break the peace. "They are not malicious, just...lost." She didn't know how to describe how she felt.

Alex shrugged off her hand and turned to glare at her. His affinity for the earth was a part of his magic and formed a dozen tiny dust devils behind him. "What do you mean?"

"They are seeking something. A way to come together."

Alex huffed and crossed his arms. "How do you know that?"

She closed her eyes for a moment to feel the magic and then opened them. "They yearn. They mindlessly seek connection because of that yearning."

"How do we stop them from destroying everything? We won't

get help for a while." Alex bit his lip and he seemed so desperate for her to have a solution that would prevent the Meeps from burning down his home. What did she know?

The Meeps' rapid desire to come together could be a geas. That type of magic would force the Meeps together. To what purpose could only be revealed when they were successful. Perhaps if she gave them a protected space, the Meeps would move on to the next step. A step which hopefully was not burning down the Archive.

"I think we give them a place to gather. Clear out this space." She gestured to the area the Meeps were already coming into and a section between the shelves.

"Is this wise?" He studied her face and slowly uncrossed his arms.

She had no idea if this plan would work, but she did know taking this tactic was more in keeping with her own magical strengths. She nodded and straightened her shoulder to give Alex confidence that she knew what she was doing. "Worst case I can use the circle to trap them until help comes."

He took a shuddery breath. "What can I do?"

"I need quick-drying paint and a clear space. I will need you to be a part of the spell." The last she had said without thought, but as the words left her lips, she knew them to be true. She needed to create a special spell circle and bring Alex into the circle's magic.

"What! Why me?" He took a small step back, and the dust devils behind him merged into something bigger.

"I think they seek protection, and that is what you do."

Alex swallowed and nodded. He moved away as more Meeps tumbled out of the wall. A few moments later, he handed her a smaller brush and a small can of green paint. Hopefully with such a small brush, the can would contain enough paint to finish the circle. Green would be a good color for her plan. She wanted to not only contain them but calm them down and bring them together. Without a word, he picked up and tucked away random objects on the floor.

"If I clear out from here to the wall, is that big enough?"

"Should be." She dipped the brush in the green paint and started the outer ring of the spell circle. The brush made a line thinner than her thumb's first joint. The Meeps gathered mostly in the center away from where she envisioned the outer ring. She worked her way around the room. Alex moved gingerly amongst the Meeps within the circle. They rubbed up against his legs as he cleaned the area. Now that he was near, there was no sneezing or exploding.

Once she closed the circle, she shuffle-stepped to the center. She drew another smaller circle in the middle. The Meeps sniffed at her, but she gently kept them away from the wet paint. For something considered a menace, the Meeps were affectionate. They rubbed their faces on her or licked her wrist. When she was done painting, the can only had a few splashes of paint left. She closed her eyes and cast a simple calling spell on the inner circle.

Hundreds of pairs of swirling purple eyes oriented on her, and the Meeps scampered closer. A steady stream of Meeps tumbled out from the wall and headed her way, swelling the ranks in the circle.

Valeria set down the brush and paint can behind her as she sat just outside the outer circle. She patted the spot next to her. "Come sit with me."

Alex sat next to her. "What are we going to do?"

"We just need to give the Meeps a safe place to gather." Valeria ignored her knotting stomach. If her hunch was right, this action would save the Archive from a fiery fate.

When she offered her hand, Alex let out his breath and took it.

"Try to relax. Watch them and look for patterns. They won't wander away because of the spell. I will reach out to you with my magic."

Alex nodded. "I don't have much."

"Your magic is all nature-based, especially of the earth. Deep inside, you protect."

Valeria sent a thread of magic to Alex. Since she and Alex were not bound in anything except new friendship, the thread had a harder time connecting. She added a little more power to the attempt before she was able to feel him.

To her senses, Alex seemed earthy, solid, and deep. She combined their magic to call to the Meeps she could still sense in the walls. Hopefully, when they were all within the circle, the geas would break.

She settled back and waited.

With luck, when the Meeps were gathered, she could help them find what they were looking for without burning down the Archive.

3

WREN

"Of all the insufferable things in the world, you had to pick a dog to bring to the Rookery." Wren said the words in his head, loudly as he always did when he had a strong reaction to something. He purposefully loosened his tense muscles in his shoulders. This was not the time nor the place to say such a thing. He had a dozen slots to fill in his program that would train those with even a spark of natural talent to make the best use of the magic they had.

The young human, Rye, clutched a small, black dog in her lap. She licked her lips and her gaze darted around the room. As she sat in the chair by his desk, he tested her magic. She had the tiniest spark. With training, she might be able to fuse and connect small items. Her magic might even bond mates' souls together into a soul-bond.

Soul mating was rare and often took a bit of magic, like Rye's, for everything to line up. The potential mates both had to be available, of the right age, and willing to bond. If they bound, the connection meant power. The mated couple would be unable to be away from their mate for long periods of time. The death of one caused the other to sicken and die. Some said the deceased soul waited nearby, unable to leave without their mate.

Her magic was not useful in the way he usually looked for, but Rye had been brave enough to enter the Rookery and apply for the program. The limp brown hair, hollowed cheeks, and dark circles under her brown eyes told the story of how she'd gotten here. The bruising on her arms and the way the dog in her lap watched the room said where she had come from.

Only one space remained in the program. The rest of the candidates were pampered kids from nearby clans. They would be fine until next year when they could apply again. This girl would not survive. Despite her weak magic, he wanted to let her stay.

Wren let his breath out through his mouth and leaned forward to make a note on his pad. He couldn't allow dogs in the roost. The last time he'd tried, the Rookery had almost lost a clutch of eggs. Joshua owed him a favor, so maybe he would have a safe place for the dog.

"Can you help me?" Rye's soft, meek voice floated to him. The dog in her arms kept a wary eye on Wren. The tail thumped hard against the leg of the chair. His nose lifted, and his body quivered.

Wren made his decision. He resisted the urge to hug Rye. Maybe after the program started, they would be on friendly terms, and he could offer his sympathy. For now, he could welcome her to the program. He added another note and nodded. "There is room in the Rookery for you."

Her mouth parted in surprise, and her eyes lit up.

"You cannot bring the dog."

She swallowed. The light dimmed from her expression. "I-I

have to get rid of Blackie?"

"I will find a temporary home for him while you are here." Wren knew that was the best course of action. Most dogs and birds didn't do well together. Blackie had the look of a mischief-maker. He was a dog after all. He didn't need anything else going wrong.

She hugged the dog closer. Her eyes shimmered, and she bit her lip. "I-I think I need to find somewhere else." Her voice wavered at the end.

Wren didn't say anything, but his stomach turned. He knew that she had nowhere to go and that if she did go back to her old neighborhood, the people there would either run her out or give her the worst jobs to do. She had no real skills. Nothing she could trade with other areas. No one to protect her. If she left here, both she and the dog would probably die. *Damn it.* That was not acceptable.

"He's just as alone as I am. And he saved my life. Without him I would be dead. I would do anything to keep him safe." She whispered the last words. The dog licked the tears from her cheek.

Rye wiped her eyes and stood, letting the dog slip from her lap. "T-thank you, but I have to go now."

Her words made his stomach drop. She was not refusing his offer for the show. The dog had saved her, and she was loyal. He understood and respected loyalty. So few people had loyalty these days. There was no other option--he'd have to allow that dog into his home.

Wren closed his eyes and sighed. "Rye, you can keep the dog, but he will need to come in for training."

She glanced away. "Are you sure?"

Wren nodded. Blackie was going to be a headache, but Wren couldn't refuse to help the poor girl. They were a package deal.

"Thank you." If anything, her tears increased, and complex

emotions rolled across her face. The dog whined softly, and the girl seemed to pull herself together. She gave Wren a hesitant smile.

He motioned to his assistant to lead Rye to her nest below. She would be fed and left to get settled in. Tomorrow, he would figure out what to do with her and her dog.

Once Wren's office door was shut and silence surrounded him, he stared at his desk. Rye was the last of the candidates for today. Restless energy coursed through him. Time ticked away, and he was no closer to saving his sister. Alesia refused to see him the last time he had tried. His friend Walter had prevented Wren from sleepwalking into his burrow and had protected Wren until he woke up.

His face heated in embarrassment at the memory. He'd been asleep, dreaming of his sister, when he'd woken up on Walter's doorstep. Wren had no idea how he had gotten there. After that morning, he magically locked his door at night. This was getting ridiculous and dangerous.

His only recourse was to solve the prophecy.

Son and daughter of the saviors of fenix

Were the son and daughter him and his sister?

Time runs out to repair

that which was sundered after the Merge

He had no idea what was broken after the Merge. But by all accounts, there were many things that were broken. Families, cities, houses. Heck, there were whole species that didn't survive the Merge.

Isolate the pair until first light on her day of birth

The only reason he allowed his sister to be with Walter was because of this line of the prophecy. Alesia with her possessed eyes had told Wren that the time had come for them to be apart. Walter was the only person Wren trusted with her life.

Wren hated being separated from his twin. Hated that he

couldn't see his friend without getting into a fight. Hated that he had made no progress in determining what to do. Defeat weighed him down, making his chest ache.

The only other line that made any sense was *Only a bound witch can save them all.*

Witches were not easy to find in this town. Few witches were interested in working with mages, let alone form a bond with one. There were many types of bonds. Maybe he only needed to be friends with a witch. The sour taste in his mouth didn't clear with a sip of wine. He'd made his nest with his actions the day Alesia was cursed like his grandmother.

Madam Red's words about Alesia's thirtieth birthday haunted him. Her birthday was just over two days away on Primus 3. He'd made almost no progress in the fourteen years he'd had to solve the prophecy.

His thoughts were interrupted when a messenger bird shrieked and landed on the incoming mail railing in his office window. The falcon wore the silver and blue colors of the Archive. The bright red of the paper drew his gaze. This was urgent. He snatched the message and gave the bird a treat.

The envelope opened at his touch, and a torn piece of red paper had the words *The archive is under attack by Meeps* scrawled out in Alex's writing. He must have sent for other reinforcements himself. The Archive would need as many mages as they could get to combat the Meeps. Meeps were as cute as they were deadly. A horde of them could burn down the city.

Wren grabbed his sword, strapped on his armor, and took to the skies. He headed past the river to the east side of town. His personal guards followed.

The Archive resembled a low storage building. But beneath that shabby exterior was the cumulative knowledge that had been saved and acquired after the Merge. His own ancestors had contributed magic to the Archive's survival. Alex had even hinted that there was a room the Aeros kept. However, anytime Wren asked after the room, Alex dodged.

Wren landed in front of the building and strode inside. Bright orange carpet assaulted his eyes. He squinted at the gray-haired woman mostly concealed behind the wooden desk. Dust and the smell of mothballs hung in the air.

"Madam." He bowed to the one demon he trusted. Why was she here and not helping with the Meeps? Perhaps the Meeps were in an odd area and he needed her guidance to reach them?

"Wren. Alex is needing you at the back of the main library." Her voice was a throaty purr. The normalcy of her voice paused him, and a trickle of unease fluffed the feathers on his back. He'd expected panic or at least concern from the demon guardian, but she wasn't showing signs of either emotion. How odd and worrying.

"Will you be helping?"

Her eyes glinted red, and she smirked. "No, that would not be wise, but you do need to hurry. Just you."

Her look sent a chill down his spine and lifted more feathers. Something other than an attack on the Archive was happening. He'd never known her to be wrong. Protective magic oozed from her aura.

Wren nodded to his men to stay and guard. He flung open the door and ran down the aisle between the shelves stacked high with priceless artifacts. The faint scent of smoke filtered to him. Loud meeps came from the back and got louder as he ran. Based on the sounds, there must be a thousand Meeps. That was enough power to burn the whole city down. His pulse raced. Where were the other mages? He'd have very little chance of containing a swarm of this size, let alone keep the Archive intact. His stomach rolled. How many artifacts would be lost?

He rounded the corner, his hands raised with the first swath of power readied, but the words to unleash the magic died on his lips. Instead of a line of magic users or warriors fighting the swarm, two people sat on the ground and a soft, warm, golden glow filled the room.

He skidded to a halt just behind a dark-haired woman who held a blond man's hand. The slight-framed man had to be Alex. Wren had never seen the woman before. He flipped on his mage sight and gasped. The magic that floated around her was one hundred percent witch. A mix of elemental and protective magic pulsed through her aura. He squinted against the bright power. He'd never seen one more formidable.

The prophecy's line popped into his mind.

Only a bound witch can save them all

And here was not only a witch, but the most powerful he had ever seen or ever heard about. The Archive's demon guardian's words made more sense.

The spell in progress glowed with—was that divination? Why would they need to look into the future? What in the world were they doing? Nothing in the magical signature said the spell would harm the Meeps or really even contain them.

He stepped closer and could just see over their shoulders. Alex and the witch were on the edge of a faintly glowing spell circle. A pile of Meeps cuddled in the middle of the circle, grooming each other. More Meeps slithered and fell out of the holes in the walls. They scurried over to the others. None of them burst into flames as they usually did. Maybe these Meeps were different. He caught sight of the burn marks on the floor by the wall and realized that whatever spell the witch was performing seemed to be preventing them from exploding.

A feeling of anticipation built in the room. As the magic built, the impression of an ancient spell wove its way between the Meeps. The power the witch supplied seemed to be revealing the dormant spell.

"We need just a little more magic," the woman said softly. A trickle of sweat fell down her face to her neck. Her hand tremored.

Even though she hadn't addressed Wren by name or turned toward him, he knew the words were to him. Wren let out a breath. Allowing even a temporary spell connection was a dangerous gamble for a mage. The fact that Alex had been willing to connect spoke well for the witch, but giving her access to his power was not something he would normally do. He'd never been able to get a witch to work with him. Perhaps this was the opportunity he needed to have access to a powerful witch.

He should demand payment in advance, but he could see the spell wavering, and he really did not want the Archive or the city to burn.

Wren settled next to the witch and took her hand. He closed his eyes and reached his magic out to Alex and the witch's spell connection. The connection took more power than he liked to establish. The woman was a stranger, after all, so that fact was not shocking. A magic user trained young to develop protections against being infiltrated. He gently added his own magic to the connection and fed his power for her to direct.

She gasped, and the feeling in the room heightened. His magic twisted and wove together with hers. He concentrated on keeping the power steady instead of worrying about what she was doing. Whatever the spell, the magic seemed to be working at containing the Meeps.

The dormant spell snapped on and everything stilled. A Meep cut off mid call and the subtle sound of claws scraping on scales and stone vanished.

The silence had him opening his eyes. Instead of a wriggling pile of Meeps, a three-foot-wide, purple, scaled egg sat in the middle of the spell circle. Wren's muscles tensed in surprise.

"Is that a dragon egg?" Alex's quiet voice asked.

4

———

VALERIA

<u>Mid-morning, Primum first, 300 years post-Merge</u>

Valeria wretched her gaze away from the newly formed egg and glanced at the man who had helped her. The egg would take a while to hatch so she could deal with it later. Her magic had not been enough to help the Meeps. Once the geas broke, the dormant spell required a substantial amount of power and the stabilizing element Alex brought. The man had supplied the extra raw energy.

The man's anger and readiness to fight had invaded her senses as he had entered the room. He must have stalked into the room, not because she had actually seen him, but because of the energy he brought. Now that she looked at him, he was not at all what she had expected.

Fancy, silver armor covered his chest, and chain links covered his arms. Large white wings fluttered behind him. The red-tipped, white feather crest on his head raised. She'd never seen an Aeros in person. His brown eyes glittered with equal parts intelligence and confusion. His only other adornment was a golden bracelet on his left arm. He controlled his strong aura, keeping the magic wrapped tight around his body. The fact that he still had power after what he contributed to the spell meant he was one of the strongest mages she knew of.

"Where are my manners? Wren, this is Valeria. Valeria, this is Wren." Alex's voice sounded thin and worn.

Wren smiled at her and kissed her hand. "Charmed." The move felt fake.

"This really is quite fascinating. There have not been any sightings of dragons since the Merge. They were listed as a species that had died with that event. Dragons, Rocs, Phoenix, and Hippocampus were the biggest species to not survive. Although since Hippocampus live in the ocean, I am not sure how anyone could tell if they were truly gone." Alex traced the patterns of the egg with his fingertips. His nervous chatter could indicate he sensed the tension between Valeria and Wren.

"What does it mean that those species are gone from this world?" Wren asked.

Alex's shoulders relaxed, and he tapped his lips. "Dragons were known as protectors. So we have a line of champions in fighting evil that would be missing from the world."

Valeria watched them interact and guessed Wren had asked the question to put Alex at ease, which in turn made her like Wren a bit better. "Is that why we have so many undead and such?"

Alex tilted his head. "Maybe."

"What about phoenixes and the rest of the creatures you listed?" Wren grabbed a broom and started sweeping.

Valeria sat at the edge of the circle and began the process to clean the green paint off the floor. The action was not only useful but let her watch Wren and Alex interact.

"Phoenixes are known for renewal and restoring barriers." Alex glanced at the egg again.

"Wait, the Merge happened because a phoenix didn't get reborn?" Wren paused his sweeping to look at Alex.

Alex shrugged and ran his hand along the egg. "The Merge could be linked to a phoenix. My best guess is that every time the phoenix was reborn, that act reinforced the layers between the worlds."

"You said worlds. How many are there?" Wren started sweeping again.

"The human world and the world of myth merged. There is a spirit or ghost world that lays right on top of this one. There is a demon realm, sometimes called the Abyss, and maybe a realm of gods. We are not sure how many there are. In fact—"

"We need to have an in-depth conversation after you do some research, but for now, what do we have to do with the dragon egg and to clean this up?" Wren gestured toward the pile of shed scales and fuzz that he had swept together.

Alex blinked and then his cheeks heated. "Clean up. Yes. Thank you for coming to help. Where are the others? I should thank them too." Alex fidgeted back and forth and wrung his hands together. Small dust devils formed behind him.

Wren leaned his broom against a shelf and fished out a piece of paper. He handed the red paper to Alex.

"That's odd. The note I gave to the guardian asked you to bring reinforcements." Alex frowned at the paper in his hands.

Valeria's instincts flared. She was meant to meet Wren. If the others had come, she would not feel indebted to Wren for helping with the Meeps. Had he brought others, not only would the spell have been a bigger group effort, but a bigger group might have jumped in and attacked the Meeps without warning. Once attacked, the Meeps would have exploded again. She shuddered. With the bigger group, flaming Meeps were far more likely to happen.

"You need to find out how to care for a dragon egg and write up how to deal with Meeps for the other cities." Wren's smile was kind and seemed faintly indulgent. Wren and Alex must be true friends.

Alex sighed. "Yes. The care of the dragon egg would be much more important."

Valeria stood and reached to feel the egg. A tiny life pulsed with her senses. "The dragon is fine for now."

Wren's feathers shifted. Was that nervousness? He smiled at her, but the smile was a fake smile that did not reach his eyes. "I'd like to hire you for an issue I have been having."

"I'm not looking for a job." She glanced at Alex, but he seemed to be fascinated with the egg. Was he really, or was he trying to ignore what was going on between them? Witches did not work with mages. A mage could not keep their contempt in check, which would in turn affect the witches' more feelings-based magic.

"I would be willing to pay handsomely for your time." No amount of money in the world would keep her sister and baby safe. Not unless there was some way to hide them from the demons' senses.

"I don't need money. Thank you, but I'm not interested."

"What do you need? I would consider this a personal favor." The look on his face said that he would give her whatever she asked for. Not because she was important but because whatever was going on meant that much to him. The last part of his statement was probably meant to make her feel the debt she owed him for borrowing his magic.

If she were to work with him, what would she want? Hiding was not a long term solution, but that tactic could help until she could break the family curse or deal with Isabella. "Conceal-ment. The good kind." Valeria lifted her chin.

"I can do that. Concealment works better if I know what I am concealing against."

His comment made sense. A general concealment would be just that, but one specific to a species or magical type would allow much better coverage. "Demons."

Wren nodded. "That is well within my capabilities."

"Two," Valeria said. "If I work with you, I need two charms." Those would protect her sister and future baby. If Corona wore a charm while she was pregnant, the baby would be protected until after the baby was born. They could slip the other charm on right away to protect them both. No one was sure when or how the demon soul was combined with the baby's soul.

"I will get you what you need if you help me." She believed he would do whatever actions and sacrifices needed to solve his problem.

"Tell me about your issue."

"One of the people at the Rookery is under a curse and needs a witch to break the spell." Something about the way he gave her the facts set her on edge. The issue was more than that he was being vague, but like he was purposely leaving huge things out of the story. One generic person did not reflect the depth of feeling and commitment he had for the specific person.

"I will need more information to be able to help." She watched him carefully to see if he would give her more clues.

"I can give you more details when you move into the Rookery."

Had she heard him wrong? "Move in?"

"Of course, so we can work closely together. The Rookery has magical protections, just as the Archive does." Wren sounded so matter-of-fact it was as if it were a forgone conclu-sion that she would work with him.

His words set her even more on edge. She would be leaving the safety and more importantly, the staggering knowledge contained within the Archive to follow a mage she had just met to his home. Alex seemed to be friends with him, which was a positive thing, but Alex had not mentioned Wren before now, nor had he supplied any details of their relationship.

"I need some time to think about your offer." She backed away from Wren. The painted lines could be removed later. The magic within them was dispersed, so the spell circle wouldn't cause any issues.

Wren nodded, but his face twisted with what looked like annoyance. "Do you know where the Rookery is?"

"Yes."

"Give them your name at the gate, and they will let you in." Wren picked up the broom and started sweeping again. His sweeps were rougher, kicking up a bit of dust on the stroke.

Alex had his lip in his teeth, and he looked the perfect picture of worry. "Be careful."

Valeria nodded and gripped Alex's arm.

The urge to flee had her feet moving. She raced out of the Archive. Being away from Wren didn't make her feel any better. She wandered through the city, making sure to keep her disguise in place.

The scent of cinnamon and freshly baked bread drew her from her circling thoughts and reminded her of the first time using her human magic. That familiar smell hung in the air of the West Market. Brightly colored fabric fluttered in the gentle breeze in the lane between stone buildings. Jubilant people filled the narrow passage. They talked and laughed and interacted as if they were not weighed down by worry.

If only she were so lucky. She'd been so dumb to leave the safety of the Archives. Alex had shown himself to be a good friend, and being out in the open was stupid. The absurdly attractive Wren could hold the key to saving her sister and her unborn child. Valeria knew why she had panicked. For all his charm, Wren had been lying or at the very least hiding something big. Secrets were akin to lies. Her grandmother's lie had almost cost Valeria and her sister's lives. She was done with secrets. She'd find some other way to save Corona and her baby.

A glint of light and movement across the way caught her attention. She stepped closer and realized that the light was a spider web woven into a wooden frame. The threads glistened in the sun. Some threads hung down with beads and red-tipped white feathers. A faint aura of peace hung on the frame. The tag next to the item declared the art a dream protector. The note said that the spiky bad dreams would be caught by the sticky spider web. Only the good dreams would drip down the feather.

If only a simple spell and construct were what brought good dreams. Valeria shivered. Spider webs had never heralded good things in her life. The feather reminded her of Wren's head crest and his offer. The dream protector made her feel like Wren was trapped in a web not of his own making just as she had been with her birth family. All of these thoughts were odd considering she'd only met Wren once and had run away from that meeting.

Was it a sign from the Goddess? Her estranged family, Valeria's aunts and Isabella, were still loose in the world. Valeria and Corona represented two of the few beings who had ever escaped from demon-possessed families.

Her skin crawled. The sight of the tattoos on her skin calmed her. At least she would be protected against being possessed again. The tattoos were a blessing that had ousted the demon trying to take over her body. Neither Corona nor the baby had such tattoos and probably would not be able to get them. The power required for her tattoos came from the death of her cousin. She closed her eyes to suppress that memory.

A sense of unease caused her to look to her right.

A woman looking at her from two stalls over seemed familiar. The dark eyes, skin, and hair didn't nudge a memory, but the way she moved did. That was odd. Maybe there was more to the woman than Valeria could see right now.

She activated the true sight tattoo on her left shoulder blade with a tiny push of magical energy. With a faint scent of cinnamon, the world shimmered around her and then cleared.

The dark skinned woman no longer stood there. Instead, Isabella with her pale skin, deep red lips, and dark red eyes touched fabric in the stall.

Valeria sucked in a breath and tried to push down the rising panic. Just because Isabella was here didn't mean she had noticed Valeria. As if she heard her thoughts, Isabella gazed directly at her and smirked.

Valeria's heart pounded. That expression made her feel like a little girl about to receive a punishment from Isabella for not making her happy. Valeria hadn't known then that only her death would ever make her grandmother happy.

Valeria hid her reaction and lifted her chin. She let her own smile out trying to picture hunting Isabella down and finally ending her reign of terror.

I have no idea how to or how to save my family.

Isabella's smirk only got bigger.

Valeria backed away into the dream protector. The sticky web moved when she moved her head.

"You will have to pay for that." The merchant, a tall, skinny human, waved a finger at her.

"Just a moment." She freed her hair, but when she looked up, Isabella was gone.

Good Goddess.

Valeria scanned the crowd for Isabella or her aunts. She didn't see any of her old family. She wasn't sure if that was a good or a bad thing. There were plenty of ways to follow someone, from spells to hiring a kid to watch them. The kid might even be a cousin she'd never met. Demons and demonic spells could hide deep within someone. If they were not actively controlling the person, possession was hard to magically see.

Valeria bit her lip. Panic-running didn't make any sense. She needed to plan her next move, or she could end up falling directly into Isabella's hands. She would have to avoid this market for the foreseeable future. If she were careful, she could lose whatever tail she could have following her.

She paid for the trinket her hair had ruined and headed deeper into the crowd. Once she was out of the fair, she funneled her fear and worry into a snap of magical energy. On the next turn, she would dart to the darkness on the alley she knew was around the corner and activate her hiding tattoo. Then she could see if anyone or anything followed her.

She darted around the corner and crouched in the alley with the hiding spell in place. Unless the person had true sight, Valeria would disappear from normal vision and most magical spells. She gazed back through the crowd looking for any indication that someone had seen her disappear or could still see her. No one seemed to notice her or her disappearance.

She knew now that time was running out before Isabella and her aunts found her again. Unfortunately, she still had no more idea what to do about them than she had when she had first escaped. Adding on the extra pressure of her sister and her unborn niece meant perhaps she had to chance Wren's offer. At the very least, she would have protection amulets for her trouble.

Valeria waited a few minutes to be sure no one noticed her and then, still invisible, she headed toward Wren's home. She stayed on the side of the road where there were less people. The trip took far longer than it should have. She paused dozens of times and hid in the shadows to make sure she was not followed. After an hour, she approached the Rookery.

The building towered above her. Valeria straightened her shoulders and walked to the gate to knock. Hopefully, she was not making a terrible mistake.

5
———

WREN

<u>Noon, Primum first, 300 years post-Merge</u>

Wren opened the door to the guest room on the ninety-eighth floor of the Rookery. The chamber should be saved for visiting royalty or close friends, but it felt right to have Valeria in this location. After all, she would be the one who helped save his sister.

"It's beautiful." Valeria glanced around and tucked her bag next to the door.

"I'd like to start right away. We are under a deadline." Wren leaned against the open doorway.

She walked to the window and peeked out. "Why not start with telling me what is really happening?"

Even though her body language had not changed, she looked as if this were a test, and if he didn't pass, she would be gone again. Saving his sister was too important. He needed to tell her the truth. He rubbed his head feathers down. "We have a prophecy."

. . .

Son and daughter of the saviors of fenix
Time runs out to repair
that which was sundered after the Merge
Isolate the pair until first light on her day of birth
Seek the kept flame and release
Two halves united shall burn and be reborn
Only a bound witch can save them all
Or the immortal shall die
and break open fully the portal to the Abyss.

"Does the prophecy mean anything to you?" Valeria asked.

Nerves skittered up his spine. This was too vital for him to be showing so much emotion. He let out a quiet breath, unclenched his hands, and worked to flatten his head feathers. "No. I have researched what I could. The terms are too vague."

"All parts of a prophecy are important. The truth comes from understanding the whole. What does fenix mean?"

"Old Earth Latin for phoenix." That fact was one of the first things he had found. Not that phoenix made any sense on the surface. What could his family have to do with a phoenix?

"Phoenix? Is that why you have a phoenix as your house emblem?" Valeria frowned, and her gaze darted around the room.

The question brought Wren out of his reverie. His family had no house emblem. "What?"

"You have phoenixes on some of the doorway mantels." She turned from the window and focused her gaze on him.

Wren tried to puzzle out what she was saying, but her words made no sense. Witches had a reputation amongst mages as not being grounded or practical. "We do not."

Valeria tilted her head, seeming to study him. She pulled him over to her room's door and pointed to the lintel above the doorway. The repeating designs were the same ones over most of the doors in the Rookery. "See it here?"

"No." The design contained nothing but swirls.

Valeria closed her eyes, and a flash of magic stunned him. Some of the swirls highlighted and the stylized pattern of a phoenix appeared. Wings outstretched, the phoenix appeared to fly.

Wren's stomach fluttered as he ran his fingertip along the pattern. Warmth flared up his finger and along his arm. "You've seen more of these? Here in the Rookery?"

Valeria nodded. "On every doorway and carved into the chair rail of the halls. How did they get here?"

"My grandmother. She was the one who finished the tower before she died." Wren's stomach churned. He didn't want to think about his grandmother or her brother and their fiery deaths.

Valeria touched his arm but asked no questions. He could see the curiosity in the set of her shoulders and the sparkle in her eyes. "The images must be a clue. Maybe the pictures tell a story?"

"Why couldn't I see them before? Were they hidden by magic?" Wren ran his finger along the swirl again. Were they even cut into the stone?

"No. I just highlighted the image so you could see them."

Having phoenixes on the walls was just another puzzle piece. Maybe. "How does this help me?"

"No idea. Let's look." She took his hand and tugged him into the hallway. Her touch sent a small bolt of awareness through him that he ignored. She gestured to the top of the hall.

He looked up and squinted. "Are they flying in the same direction?"

"Yes, they are all heading that way." She pointed down the hall. "Let's follow them."

For a moment, the hesitant, solemn woman was replaced by a mischievous child. She tugged his hand again. He let her lead him down the hall and up the stairs to the level that the family lived on. How had he missed so many phoenixes? When she stopped suddenly, he almost ran into her.

"What's wrong?"

She released her hold on him and waved between where they had come to the panel in front of them. "They roost here." She pointed down the other hall. "Those phoenixes are flying here and those over there fly here as well and then roost."

"What does it mean?"

She shook her head. "No idea. But the path leads here. The prophecy said *Isolate the pair until first light on her day of birth.* I'm not sure that this is the pair, but the fact that there are two may be significant."

"There are two phoenixes. That one is flaming, and the other one is not." The desire to touch had him reach for the stone. Before he could make contact, he pulled his hand away and stuck it behind his back. Mages shouldn't just touch things because they felt like they wanted to.

She patted his arm. "Tell me what just happened?"

"I wanted to touch each bird at the same time. I wanted to feel them under my fingers." Mages didn't give into feelings. Logic controlled his magic. He should be over those impulses.

She gave him a puzzled frown. "Why didn't you?"

How could he explain the complex mess in his head? "That desire is silly."

She tilted her head and patted his arm again. "You've been ignoring your gut when dealing with the prophecy. Maybe that is the issue. If you feel like you ought to touch both, then do so. And touch them the way your gut tells you to."

Wren's face flamed with embarrassment. This was stupid. He had important things to do.

"Let me ask you this. What does it hurt to try? You have no other leads." If Valeria's voice hadn't been so even, he might have let loose his anger and frustration. But her tone soothed him. He had no other leads. She was right. What did it hurt to try? A witch would certainly not judge him for his emotions.

He faced the wall and shook out his shoulders. The two phoenixes were different yet the same. They had the same whimsical feel, but the first seemed to be on fire, the second not. The depth of the image was different. The one that didn't seem to be on fire had shallower lines that reminded him of a spirit or ghost.

He closed his eyes and then moved his hands forward until his hand placement felt right. Then he pressed them into the wall. A flash of heat and magic traveled up both arms, and the room shook.

When he blinked his eyes open, he no longer saw the wall in the Rookery. Plaster walls with rounded shelving dominated the room. The blanket on the nest was royal purple with mountains stitched into the middle. He was in his old bedroom in the mountain castle. His room that had been gone for years was still decorated in his childhood colors.

A sharp tug of magic in his chest pulsed. He resisted the pull, seeking to see who was calling. The request didn't have the imperious edge that his father's summons had nor the impatient feel of a tutor. The person calling him was related, but the call felt different. Urgent.

Curious now, he followed the pull out of his room and down

the hall that would lead to the family section of the castle. The detail of his surroundings and the feel of the floor on his feet could mean this was a triggered memory. The magic could have broken a blocked memory, or the magic could be keyed to this particular memory. This was the first clue he'd had for years. He sunk deeper into the memory.

He passed the opened doors of the other empty nests. The slight snuff of the hobgoblins echoed out. They kept the rooms clean, rooted out vermin, and guarded the space.

The number of royalty dwindled over the years. The family now only occupied four rooms in this wing. His, his sister Alesia's, his father's, and his grandmother's brother's. The pull was from the very last room in the section. His grand-uncle's room.

The closed door gave no hint as to the contents of the room. Wren knocked, but heard nothing. If not for the still urgent pull from the room, he would have left. A chill swept down his back. The last time he had seen his grand-uncle was years ago. Grand-uncle'd quarreled with Wren's father. Grand-uncle had seemed so cold, but his eyes had been molten with emotion.

Another shiver coursed down Wren's back at the memory, raising feathers. Grand-uncle's eyes had been a combination of rage and grief. His grief was so powerful, the emotion thrummed in the air around him.

Wren pushed open the door, revealing a darkened room. The smell of old feathers and a room gone too long without cleaning assaulted his nose.

He sneezed.

A chuckle sounded from the middle of the room. "Come in, boy."

Wren entered and the door shut behind him, cutting off the light. A faint red glow flickered in the nest.

A few more hesitant steps brought Wren to the side of the sleeping area. The blanket in the middle moved. A wave of heat drifted his way.

Did he imagine the reddish light that flickered in the darkness?

A mage light flipped on by the bed. His grand-uncle lay in his nest. Red eyes with gray pupils glared from the old man's wrinkled face. The lines around Grand-uncle's mouth betrayed pain and bitterness. A white head crest feather fell and landed in the nest. His grand-uncle should not be molting now.

Had there been a reddish glow around his grand-uncle's skin and feathers? He searched his mind trying to come up with an explanation that made any sense. The light had flickered as if his grand-uncle had been on fire, but clearly he was not.

"Your father was not going to tell you," his grand-uncle croaked out. He cleared his throat.

"Tell me what?"

"About the curse."

Wren rocked back on his heels. He'd read everything he could get his hands on about the family. All of the books had said that the Aero's royalty had been prosperous. The books had implied that the Merge had somehow hurt the royal family. But there had been nothing about a curse.

"Tell me more, Grand-uncle."

His grand-uncle chuckled. "What did you see when you walked in?"

His question was a test. "A flickering red light that looked like there was fire within the chamber."

His grand-uncle nodded. "Do they talk about your grandmother?"

Wren wasn't sure what to say. There were whispers that she had gone mad. "Only that she died young."

"They say more than that, so don't spare my feelings." His grand-uncle's voice whipped in command far stronger than his body looked to be capable of.

"They say she was touched and set herself and most of the castle on fire." Wren watched his grandfather carefully. The gossip also told of the strange dynamic between the siblings. Some had even said that Grandmother's death was Grand-uncle's fault.

His grand-uncle sighed. "She did set herself and much of the old wing on fire. That much is true, but her actions were not because she was touched. She wanted to save us...to save me."

Grand-uncle's words sent a shiver down his spine. "Save you from what?"

"So much has been lost. The fire burns hotter now and will pass on, and so will the curse." The old man paused to take a ragged breath.

"I don't understand." Unease twisted his stomach at the wildness in Grand-uncle's gaze.

"You and Alesia are in danger."

Wren's thoughts stopped. He looked at his grand-uncle and saw the serious expression on his face. He was clearly worried about them.

"How do you know?" Wren asked. He thought about his bright sister. The energy and cheerfulness that was so out of place in this dour castle. The way she seemed to glow when excited. She was so different from the rest of them. From him.

"Did you know that your grandmother and I were twins?"

Wren rocked back. The urge to flee what he didn't understand was strong. Twins seemed to happen in the royal line with every other generation. The first documentation of twins happened to the queen during the Merge.

"The flame was not ready to move. Or maybe the flame was waiting for twins."

Wren shivered. His grand-uncle had always been a hard, practical mage. His words now seemed fantastical.

"What happened to Grandmother?"

His grand-uncle's gaze locked onto Wren's face. "You will be my heir."

"Please tell me what happened."

His grand-uncle sighed. "My sister could see the future. She knew that it was not yet time for the curse to be lifted."

"She became touched?" He'd heard that she'd been able to see the future because she had an extra spirit within her. She'd also been obsessed with fire.

"The day before our thirtieth birthday, she sacrificed herself for the clan." His expression turned inward. His eyes were downcast.

"What do you mean?"

"If she hadn't, everyone in our clan would have died. We are missing pieces of the prophecy. That's why I call this a family curse. The urges became too strong to fight and giving in leads to death."

Wren straightened in shock. No one had said anything about urges or his grandmother sacrificing herself. He had to be sure. "So Grandmother was not the one who set herself on fire?"

Grand-uncle closed his eyes. A tear streaked down the wrinkles on his cheek. "She did, but she sacrificed herself to save me and to give our family a chance to break the curse."

"How do we break the curse?"

Grand-uncle shook his head. "You need to be aware and prepare for when Alesia is touched. If you can't save her, she will sacrifice herself to save the clan."

"I don't understand. What am I saving her from?"

"I don't know," his grand-uncle said. He sunk back into the nest. "I did the best I could. You have to do better. Be strong. Resist the urges as long as you can."

The smell of smoke drifted to Wren's nose. A faint bit of heat surprised him. He reached forward and put his hand on his grand-uncle's forehead. His skin burned to the touch. "Grand-uncle?"

"You must find the source of the curse," his grand-uncle said without opening his eyes.

"Grand-uncle?" Wren whispered. He needed to get help. Who would be able to help? The wing was empty but for the hobgoblins. His father would be in the throne room.

Wren stood to fly his father, but the old man grabbed Wren's wrist.

Heat radiated up from the nest. Grand-uncle must have dropped a flame in his nest. Wren needed to rescue his kin. Wren pulled back, scrabbling at the floor. His grand-uncle didn't budge. If anything his grip tightened on Wren's wrist. A shiver of fear pulled at him. He could smell smoke.

Grand-uncle opened his eyes. Flamed licked within his pupils. *What the Goddess?*

Wren pulled away, but he couldn't break his kin's grip.

"Save her, or we all will die." The old man's voice was a harsh whisper.

The bedding smoked. The hand wrapped around his wrist heated.

Wren jerked back as flames suddenly appeared on his grand-uncle's arm and jumped to Wren's wrist. The flames raced up his arm to his chest. Pain radiated through his body.

He was on fire.

Someone screamed. The scream was his voice, but he felt farther from his body. The feeling of flying overtook him and then he landed hard on the floor.

He opened his eyes to see the nest engulfed with flames.

As darkness closed in, he swore he saw the image of a fiery bird roll up on the smoke.

Pain brought Wren back to the here and now. Fire engulfed his hands as he pressed them hard enough into the wall to draw blood.

6

———

VALERIA

<u>Afternoon, Primum first, 300 years post-Merge</u>

Valeria's senses flooded with magic. At first divination magic flashed as Wren froze, but then fire flared to life. She didn't dare touch him. He was meant to have this vision.

Wren muttered, "Cursed."

Strong fire-based magic rose. She sensed no hostile intent, but Wren's hands burned against the wall. Blood dripped on the lines of the two phoenixes, which seemed to activate a dormant spell.

The wall between his hands creaked open, revealing a dark passage. Old air puffed out, making her cough. The spell surrounding Wren dissipated.

Valeria grabbed him before he could fall and helped him sit on the floor in the hall.

"What just happened?" He shook in her grasp. Her sympathy

rose. Mages were taught to ignore their feelings, and now he had no real way to deal with them.

"You provoked a spell." The passage didn't trigger any of her protective spells. Wren's feathers drooped, and his eyes were bloodshot. Whatever had happened must have taken a lot of energy. He looked wrecked, but she knew he needed to move before he could think too hard. "Let me check your hands before we go in."

Healing magic was not something she did, but she knew how to bandage wounds. She flipped his hands so she could assess his palms. Smooth, unbroken skin greeted her gaze. She ran her fingers down his palm and felt the faint tingle of fire magic. Wren stared at her as if he was not really seeing her. His face was even paler than normal.

"Before we go in, I need to know what you saw in your vision." Valeria kept a hold of his hand and watched his face carefully for a reaction. The flash of divination had to have been a vision.

He winced and then closed his eyes. He told her about his memory of his grand-uncle's cryptic words, what his grand-uncle had said about his sister's death, and how he had died.

When Wren was done, he looked as if he needed a hug. Even though they had just met, she gave him one. His warm body tensed against her before he relaxed. She let out just a touch of magic to soothe him. When he stiffened in her arms again, she released him and stood up.

"Let's see what is down the secret passage."

He would not look at her as she helped him stand. He frowned both at the ground as if it were responsible for his flashback and at anything else for possibly putting him in a grumpy frame of mind.

She tugged him down the hall. Stylized phoenix sconces flickered to life as she pulled him. Ten paces in, the hall opened into a massive, circular chamber. Powerful magic thrummed inside. Everything felt purposeful, from the way the walls joined the ground to the thick feeling of the stone walls. Runes made to withstand volcano-level fires filled the walls and floor. Layer upon layer of other protective magic wove into the room. Oddly enough, the protective circle was on the side of the space, not in the middle as was typical. The golden spell circle carved into the floor looked to be able to keep a catastrophic amount of fire contained.

"What is this place?"

Wren's wide eyes made him look stunned as he spun to take in the chamber. "I don't know."

She sank her magical senses into the feel of the room. All she could sense was a faint feeling of anticipation. Could another dormant spell be in this chamber?

When she opened her eyes, she noticed a table to her left with an open book. The faint aura of preservation magic glowed around the table.

She stepped toward the book. Loopy elegant writing scrawled across the page. The name Kamali stood out at the top. "Who is Kamali?"

"Where did you see that?"

Valeria froze at the shock in Wren's voice. She gestured to the book on the table.

His body stiffened, and his expression closed. "That's none of your business."

"Tell me what is really going on." She had the faintest outline of what was happening. "Who is cursed and how? What does the curse have to do with you?"

Wren's lips pressed together.

She wasn't sure why, but she stepped forward and touched his arm. "I can only help you if I know what is going on."

Wren closed his eyes and sighed. "My sister is possessed by

the spirit I think caused my grandmother to die. My sister is the daughter in the prophecy. I think Grand-uncle meant that Alesia will set herself on fire if we can't figure out what is happening."

His words were the truth as he knew it. She could sense how much he loved his sister. That emotion was something she could understand as she felt the same way about her own sister. Valeria would guess that Wren's sister would feel the same way about him and would do anything to save him. She thought about the story of the grand-uncle and the fire Wren produced to unlock this chamber. "Your grand-uncle said your grand-mother did what she did to save him. Did he say to save him from fire?"

Wren frowned. "No. He had no details. Just talked about a curse and Grandmother choosing to save the clan."

Wren's feathers had literally risen as he talked. He didn't seem open to talking about his family anymore. "What spell did you cast to produce the fire to open this chamber?" Valeria had other things she needed to know, so she decided to switch topics.

He jerked, and his gaze filled with confusion. "I cast no spell."

"Where did the fire from your hands come from or the healing of your wounds?"

Wren opened his hands and gazed at them blankly for a long moment. "I-I don't know."

His answer was also the truth. His grand-uncle had said, "You will be my heir." Perhaps he had passed along the fire to Wren on that day. She snuck another look at Wren's closed expression. This was probably not the best time to bring up such speculation.

"Perhaps your grandmother left a clue." She gestured toward the book. "May I?"

Wren released a breath and seemed to shake himself, his

feathers fluffing and then lying flat as she watched. "Maybe she did."

"To those who come after me. I am Kamali. Only fire can do what we need to free the family from this curse. We failed to find the final piece. His urges grew too strong to resist. I did what I had to do to protect my twin and the rest of the family. I died so he might live." Valeria read the words aloud.

A feather stuck out of the top of the book marking a page. She flipped the book open. Scrawled out in neat letters was a spell to remove fire trapped within someone.

She offered the book to Wren. "Wren? I need to know what you know. Anything related to your sister or fire."

He nodded and told her about Madam Red, the line of women Madam Red had called demons, Alesia demanding they be separated, his inability to find a cooperative witch, and his own struggle with being away from Alesia, and the impending deadline.

The mention of the female demons and something about this room reminded her of the basement of the two-story house Isabella had summoned her to after Corona had "died." The connection eluded her.

Wren rubbed his eyes. "*Seek the kept flame and release* could mean that you cast the fire removal spell on me."

That phrase could mean that, but the rest still made no sense. Who was the immortal who would die, and what were the two halves? The only two things they had were the twins and the two phoenixes on the door to this chamber. None of the lines of the prophecy made any sense. Her gut said casting the spell to remove Wren's fire was not the path they needed to take.

One look at the stubborn tilt of his jaw said he thought the spell was the best next step, and he would not rest until she cast the spell. No matter what the cost.

7

———

WREN

<u>Afternoon, Primum first, 300 years post-Merge</u>

Wren followed Valeria out of the phoenix room. He needed to get a door to cover this room. The exposed magic was too much for the chamber to be open and accessible by anyone who passed it in the hall.

Valeria shot him a look as if checking his reaction. She might even be wondering how he was going to behave. He rubbed his eyes. She had a right to be uncomfortable. He had spent most of his time in her presence acting pissed or grumpy. She was one of the few people who got to see him outside of his serious political persona.

"What did you want to do next?" Valeria walked down the hall toward the stairs.

"You have an idea?"

"I know we just got here, but what if we go back to the Archive?"

Going back to the Archive could make sense. Valeria had almost run from him and, in his frustration, he had left Alex a mess to clean up. Not that Alex wasn't used to cleaning messes. He was also the best researcher and archivist the Archive had ever had. At least that was what everyone said. "You think Alex might already have researched the phoenix."

"Alex *is* very talented. I also need to check on the egg." A blush crept across her cheeks. "I may have left before making sure Alex was okay."

Even as she blushed, she still met his gaze and grinned sheepishly. He was attracted to how she owned her emotions.

A low growl caught his attention. That noise was probably that darn dog Blackie. He'd have to deal with the dog before they left.

"What is that?" Valeria tilted her head toward the stairway.

Wren sighed. "How about I meet you downstairs? I have a few things to take care of."

"You really need a spell for non-winged people to get around this tower better." Valeria cast a sideways glance at him.

Heat flooded his face. He knew there were things he could do to make the Rookery easier on the non-flying people who lived here. He just hadn't yet. No one complained. And if anyone was elderly or needed help, there were plenty of able-winged people to step in and bring them where they needed to go.

She waved her hand in dismissal. "You have enough to worry about. Besides, walking helps me think." Her implication that she was going to need to think as much as possible was left unsaid.

As Valeria walked down the stairs, Wren followed the low growl up. As he neared the floor above, Rye sat curled in a ball in the doorway. Beyond, he could see Blackie growling at one of the maids.

"What is going on here?" Wren put his best "I'm in charge" voice on.

The maid instantly snapped to attention.

The dog slunk back to Rye, still softly growling

"This animal was trying to get into your private chambers." The maid sniffed and looked down her nose at the dog and girl.

The girl wrapped her arms around the dog as he snapped at the maid.

"Thank you. I have it now." He dismissed the maid who walked away down the hall. A door slammed in the distance.

"Did you want to talk about it?" Wren sat in the stair next to the pair. The dog was far more trouble than he was worth.

"Blackie just wanted to go into your library."

She must be assigning her own desires to the dog. He didn't know a lot about dogs, but dogs didn't seem intelligent in the same way humans were.

"Oh? Why did he want that?"

She bit her lip, then shrugged and looked away. Was that embarrassment painted on her face? He let out a sigh. "How about later I will come back and spend some time with you and Blackie."

She looked down at her dog, hiding her face in his fur. Did she know how much of an annoyance the dog was turning out to be?

"But not in my room. We can meet in the training chambers."

The girl nodded. "That would be safer."

"You head back to your room, and I will see you tonight."

She nodded and carried the dog away, who watched Wren from over her shoulder. Damn dog.

He hurried to his office and sent a request to get a door installed with a heavy duty lock on the newly found room. He flew down just in time for Valeria to step off the final stair.

She huffed. Sweat dripped down one side of her red face.

A small sliver of guilt ate at him. "I could fly us to the Archive."

"Fly?" She gave him a puzzled frown "I didn't think..."

Aeros flew other people. He mentally finished her sentence. Aeros did transport people on occasion. The people who needed a rescue, like Alesia's friend Serene, or people who needed help with the stairs. Heat flared on his face, probably making it as red as hers. He wasn't even sure why he offered. "We can walk, if you would rather."

"No. I'd like to fly. I've only flown with a spell, but that spell is only for emergencies." She winked at him, making him feel better.

He carefully picked her up, bridal style, and then launched up into the air. A few flaps had him airborne. She held on tightly enough to stay stable but not enough to strangle him. If she fell, she could probably cast a spell to break her fall before she hit the ground. He headed to the south side where the Rookery's roof exit was for outbound air traffic.

He closed his eyes for a moment as the sunlight hit his face. Joy bubbled in his chest. The Rookery was the tallest building in the town. From here he could even see the edges of the town and the large rock formation that protected Walter's burrows.

The urge to see his sister pulled his flight toward Walter's home before he caught himself and corrected the course. The trip took only moments for them to land outside of the Archive.

"That was much faster, thank you." Valeria flushed but still grinned at him.

They entered the Archive. The reception area was empty. The guardian demon was not present.

"Why isn't there ever anyone at the desk?" Valeria asked.

Wren blinked. "There is a..." Demon. A demon that Valeria

would probably not take too kindly to at this moment. Since the demon guard was strong in divination, she would know when Valeria was coming and not be present. "Let's find Alex."

Cursing came from the back of the Archive's main room.

Wren found Alex kneeling, trying to remove the green paint on the floor with a rag. He rubbed the floor briskly but didn't seem to remove any paint.

"Alex, I can clean that after we check on the egg," Valeria said.

Alex sat up and then smiled at Valeria. "Thank you. That paint was not coming off."

"I may have had to put a spell on it so the Meeps wouldn't take the paint off if one exploded." Valeria said the words like a confession. She sat down by one edge of the spell circle and released the faintest trickle of magic. Then she took the brush and started scrubbing.

"That explains why I was having such a hard time removing the green," Alex muttered as he stood.

"What are the odds you were able to learn something about the phoenix?" Wren asked. The room was still a mess with the paint and pile of scales and tufts of fur.

Alex blinked at him and tilted his head. "Did they suddenly become more important?"

"Valeria discovered enough of them in the Rookery that she wondered if they were our house emblem." He made light of how offended he had been.

Valeria snorted.

"The only record I could find so far was a story about the rebirth of the phoenix being linked to positive things and protection. I saw a record that the night of the Merge a phoenix was seen blazing in the fire just before death."

"Was that normal?"

"The records are very scarce. There was a record that the human church aligned their calendar with the phoenix's 500-year life cycle," Alex said.

"And we don't have any idea what the year was when that cataclysm happened in the human world." Wren knew so much knowledge was lost with the colliding of worlds.

"Joshua knows." Alex seemed to realize that he had said something odd because he glanced away. His red cheeks reddened.

Wren would have to ask Joshua later. Maybe knowing when the phoenix was supposed to be reborn would help them discover if they were linked to the barriers between worlds being renewed.

"How do you think that works? Like there is a phoenix between each set of worlds?"

"Maybe there was one for each of the layers, and their rebirth strengthened the barriers." Alex nodded and seemed to be deep in thought. "If that were the case, there would be a phoenix for each world that touched ours."

"I'm not sure this information would be in any book." Valeria had cleaned up half of the spell circle.

"You are right. If only there was more documentation about the Merge. Maybe that would give us a clue." Alex shot his gaze to Wren and then looked away. Wren had no idea what that look meant.

"What about the dragon egg?" Alex asked. "I read that different species of egg-laying creatures have to incubate their eggs differently to keep them healthy. What do the Aeros do?"

"Aeros don't lay eggs." Wren huffed.

Alex went bright red. "S-Sorry."

"I'm sorry. You would have no way of knowing that. Our pregnant females tend to stay near their nest." Wren grabbed the broom and swept.

"Would you consider a dragon to be a bird or a lizard?" Alex stared at the floor, lost in thought. Small dust devils swirled around the outside of the room.

"Why?"

"Because birds rotate their eggs and lizards do not." Wren thought about the debates that Walter and he would get into. His chest ached. He missed his friend as much as he missed his sister.

"If we get it wrong, the egg will die?"

Valeria was up next to Alex, and she pulled him into a hug. "Shhhh. It's okay. I know some spells that can help us figure out what to do about the egg, I know the egg is important to you."

Alex hugged her back and nodded. "There's just something..."

Valeria didn't make him finish the thought but just squeezed him and released. Her interaction was so much different from what Wren had been taught. He might have pushed Alex for an answer. Valeria seemed to think that the answers would come at their own time. Wren never would have hugged Alex. Even if he understood that Alex was upset, the most Wren would do was a manly pat on the back. Thinking of Valeria in that light brought a warmth to his chest he usually got when thinking about Alesia or Walter.

Valeria released Alex and met his gaze. "Ready to find out?"

Alex blew out his breath and nodded. The dust devils were still small so he must not be that worried.

"Did you want to see?" Valeria glanced over at Wren.

"Yes, please."

"If you join your magic, you can feel what I feel." Valeria put her hand out to Wren. Connecting magic was easier with touch like this. He put in the extra effort to link to her magic. She placed her hand on the egg.

He could feel a swirl of magic and could feel how she

approached the egg. Her actions were not an interrogation, like he or another mage might do, but an invitation to play. The egg responded with some slight intelligence that felt reptilian. Valeria reached more magic out to touch the dragon. A wealth of information flowed from the spell. He knew that the egg did not need to be moved, and if the egg was moved to another room, they needed to keep the egg oriented the way that it currently was. The room did not need to be heated, but the room also could not be too cool. The egg would not hatch until the magic was ready, because the first dragon of its kind would have a quest that she had to make in order to open the way for more dragons.

Valeria moved away from the egg.

"That was..." He was not sure how to put what he was feeling in words. He'd never interacted with someone on that level before.

"Pretty cool." Valeria squeezed his hand and let him go. "No need to worry Alex. The dragon is healthy. We need to find a room for the egg to rest in that is protected and doesn't get too cold. I had the sense it would be awhile until the dragon is big enough and..." She glanced at Wren.

"It was almost as if she was waiting on something else before she could leave the egg." Wren added.

Alex came forward and put his hand on the egg and nodded. "We will look at the side rooms and see if any of them make sense. She?"

"The dragon is female," Valeria said.

Wren helped Alex with the rest of the cleaning. Alex chattered happily with Valeria about random things. Wren only felt slightly jealous of their easy camaraderie. Valeria was just a warm person and seemed to interact with everyone in a friendly, open manner.

Wren leaned the broom on the shelf and stretched his back.

Even with the sweeping, he felt oddly good. That itch just under his skin to see his sister was missing. He still loved and missed her, but this was different.

He had no idea what to make of it. Maybe he was finally cured of these odd urges.

8

VALERIA

Valeria woke from sleep to a strangely familiar sound. She sat up and pushed away the covers. Her Rookery room was sparsely populated with fancy furniture. This allowed her to see that no one was in the room with her. Had she heard a noise in the hallway?

She shifted out of the nest and padded to the door. Cold wood pressed against her ear as she listened.

The strange sound came again. The stifled whimper and harsh breath was the sound of someone crying but trying to keep quiet. As a child, Corona had woken Valeria up many times with that same sound. Her heart tugged.

She opened the door and walked down the hallway. The floors chilled her feet. She should have put on slippers, but the stifled sounds drew her. Around the next corner a small, human girl hunched on the ground. Her long brown hair covered her face.

"What are you doing here?" Valeria pitched her voice to be low and soothing.

The girl jumped up and turned around. Her jaw dropped and more tears fell down her face. She put her trembling finger to her lips in sign of "be quiet."

Valeria nodded. She let out her senses and didn't feel anything to account for the panic the girl had. Her whole body quivered with fear. The whites of her eyes showed, and she was trembling from head to toe.

The youngster stood up and tiptoed to Valeria. They wouldn't be able to have a conversation here. The girl took Valeria's hand and then led her back down the hall. She said nothing as she kept moving down the hallway. Her gaze scanned back and forth. She must be looking for a place to talk.

Valeria tugged the girl to Valeria's room. She opened her door and waved the girl in. Maybe if she closed and locked the door for extra protection, the youngster would feel safer. Valeria put up a ward that would keep everything in this room private.

"Who are you?" Valeria sat down on the fancy chair.

"I'm Rye." Rye moved to sit in the chair closest to Valeria.

Valeria waited a moment to see if Rye would tell her what was going on without prompting. As the silence stretched on, Valeria decided to start with easy questions. "Why were you in the hallways so late?"

"It's the only time I can be free." She frowned and closed her eyes, letting off a full-body shiver. "I'm so afraid all the time. But there is nothing I can do." The girl's voice cracked.

"Are you being bullied?" Valeria could see something like that happening. Rye seemed small and fragile. Potentially the perfect target for an unkind mage. Not that all mages were unkind. Wren could be kind.

Rye just stared at her seemingly unsure what to say.

Maybe the issue was not her classmates. "Is the staff a problem?"

"They don't like Blackie." Her voice was soft and hesitant, and she would not meet Valeria's eyes.

"Why's that?" Who was Blackie? Was he another student?

Rye seemed to choose her words carefully. "My dog causes trouble."

Dogs in stressful situations could cause trouble. Why would the staff not liking her dog make her cry or hide in the hallway?

"Is he making messes?" Valeria guessed.

Rye nodded solemnly.

"Is anyone else being mean? Like the other students?"

"They are fine. Wren told them to be nice. He can be scary sometimes." The girl didn't look scared when she talked about Wren. Her smile was small, but her expression was a mixture of hero worship and something sad.

"Is there someone else making you uncomfortable?"

Rye nodded her head and then leaned so their heads were closer. "But I can't tell you, or I'll be in big trouble." The whispered words and glaze of tears convinced Valeria not to push.

"Are you safe?"

Rye's hesitant nod did not leave Valeria feeling good. What could she do to give Rye a measure of protection? Maybe Valeria had a charm. She reached and pulled her satchel into her lap. The charm pocket was a side pocket just inside the main compartment. She ran her hand through the dozen small bags. Picking a charm was an intuitive thing. Since she was not exactly sure what would help Rye, Valeria waited for the item that felt right to her intuition. Gold fabric and small, green, four-leaf clovers on the fabric meant the charm was for protection and luck. "This is yours."

"What is it?" Rye reached for the small bag.

"A luck and protection charm. The charm will help guide you to safety and will protect the person wearing it."

Rye opened the little bag and pulled out a round disc. The small charm was shaped like a coin and had an image of a fuzzy dog on both sides. The charm had a loop so it could be hooked on a necklace or bracelet.

"This will help anyone? What if a demon were to steal it?" Rye asked, not taking her gaze off the charm cupped in her hand.

"This will not help a demon. Only someone good can access its powers." Why would Rye ask about demons? Maybe she had overheard Valeria talking about her own family.

"Is there a word to trigger the spell?"

"Woof," Valeria said, making sure to sound like a dog.

Rye's face split in a grin, making her look younger. "And the magic will work on whoever is wearing the charm?"

Valeria wondered what the girl was thinking. Her face was thoughtful as she lifted the charm up to examine it closer. Her reaction was odd. Valeria would check on the girl multiple times a day if she had to in order to find out what was going on. "Yes. So if you were wearing this charm and I said the magic word, it would help you."

"But if this charm was on a demon and you said the word, the magic would not help the demon?"

"No. The charm would help the nearest good creature as long as they were not too far away."

"That's a relief." Her shoulders relaxed, and she even gave a real smile that made her eyes sparkle. The girl seemed much more at ease. "This gives me hope that maybe things will all turn out okay."

"Did you want to talk about what is going on?"

The girl's face paled. "No. I can't yet, It's too dangerous. Promise me you will not try to talk about this again."

Valeria jerked back.

Rye's gaze was direct and her face serious. "Please."

Valeria sighed and then nodded. "I will not talk to you about this again. I will wait for you to tell me what's going on. Vow to me you will tell me as soon as you can."

Rye nodded. "I will tell you everything when I can."

Rye held out her hand to shake. Valeria gave Rye's hand a gentle squeeze before letting go.

"Did you want to stay here for the night?" Valeria asked.

Rye smiled and shook her head. "You can hug me here and walk me part way back."

Valeria laughed softly and enclosed the girl in a hug. Her body trembled against Valeria.

"I will wait for you to talk to me."

Rye nodded.

Valeria unlocked the spell on the door and led the girl almost back where she had found her. Rye turned and made a "wait here" motion and walked quietly away.

Valeria wasn't sure what to think about her odd interaction with Rye. Rye'd been scared but determined. The hall stayed quiet and after a few minutes, her feet ached with the cold. Her slippers still sat in her room by the nest. She must have misunderstood Rye's hand motion. She must not be coming back.

Valeria walked back to her room. A thump on the stairs made her pause. Why were so many people up this early?

Wren walked down the steps. She had never seen Wren in such a state. His feathers were fluffed. If he had been a human she would have called the style "bedhead." His robe hung loosely around his body and did not hide his bare feet or silky underclothes. His eyes were open but fixed on something behind her. And most damning that something was wrong, he'd walked down the stairs instead of flying.

She stepped to his side. "Wren?"

He shuffled toward her, but he gave no response to her words.

The feeling that something was very wrong heightened. She took his arm and shook him gently. "Wren?"

He kept moving forward as if she were not even there. He could be sleepwalking. No one had said anything about the prince being affected by that. But maybe they wouldn't because of the risk of rumors. But what if this was something more?

She let out a hint of magic, just to see if there was some other cause for the sleepwalking. Wren felt deeply asleep. Maybe deeper than he ought to be. She shivered from more than cold. Something felt off.

"Wren? Where are you going?" Valeria held his arm

"I need to see my sister." His voice was soft but higher pitched and younger sounding.

"Can I help you?" Valeria asked softly, tugging at his arm gently.

"I need to see my sister." His voice rose and sounded upset.

"Yes, I know. Can I help you?" Valeria led him back the way he had come. He didn't protest, but he twisted and pulled just a little bit at her hold.

She brought him into his room, shut, and locked the door. Not a great thing maybe for a prince to be locked away with a witch. But she had a feeling he was going to want the door locked.

Valeria would say his name and jolt him at the same time. She readied a wake-up jolt of magic. "Wren!"

He blinked at her but did not quite wake up.

Alarm shivered through her. He should have woken up. She examined him with her magic and saw a tiny sleep spell. How had she not noticed the magic beforehand? She sent a bolt to the spell and said, "Wren!"

He startled awake and blinked slowly at her. His gaze darted around the room and then landed on her. His brow furrowed in confusion. "What's going on?"

She had a moment to decide what to do. Her natural inclination was to tell him the truth, which might not go well. But she knew that the work he wanted her to do for him meant they would be forming a partnership of sorts. The bond might not be a very strong one, but it needed to feel real. Especially to her own witchy powers.

"Someone put a spell on you to keep you asleep. I found you sleepwalking."

Wren paled and then rubbed his face with his hand. "I thought..." He sighed and slumped.

"What's going on?"

"I seem to be filled with this urge to see my sister. During the day, it's easy enough for me to ignore." He grimaced as if that might not always be true. "But at night, I've started to dream of seeing Alesia."

"And you get up and try to go there?"

"Once I even made it to Walter's front door." Wren ducked his head. He seemed embarrassed maybe?

"That's dangerous." She kept her voice mild and made sure not to show any judgment in her tone.

He sighed. "Yes, it was. I had no guards, and no one knew I was gone. I didn't wake up until morning. Walter locked me in a closet for the night."

Valeria realized that more had happened than what they were saying. Knowing Wren, he had a plan to never let that happen again. "And you had a plan."

"Yes. I magically locked my door so I couldn't get out of my room. Where did you find me?"

"In the stairway," Valeria said. "Did you open the door with your magic?"

He looked over at her with a puzzled frown. "I never have before."

How long had he been doing this? "So, you magically lock yourself in your room?" Valeria repeated.

"It was either that or get tied to the bed, " Wren muttered. His face flamed red, and he wouldn't meet her gaze.

Valeria suppressed a laugh. Wren wouldn't appreciate her thinking he was cute when he was embarrassed. The idea that uptight Wren would allow someone to tie him anywhere was almost funny. The trust that sort of interaction would take didn't seem like something Wren would do.

So how did the door open? Maybe someone else knew about the lock and had removed it. Something had woken Valeria. Rye had been wandering the hall, so maybe there had been a disturbance that had woken up more people.

"Would a staff member have removed it?" Valeria subtly led Wren back to his bed. He would need to sleep, or he was going to hurt himself. His eyes already had dark circles under them, and he seemed worn.

"No, they would not have the skills."

If the culprit was not the staff, that limited the people who might have access. Before she jumped to an intruder, maybe she needed to make sure Wren himself was not the person removing the spell on the door. "Have you ever done magic while sleeping?"

Wren shook his head. "No. Mages don't generally use magic while sleeping. Something about not having access to the power the correct way."

Mages used logic and ritual to harness their powers. Dreams were chaotic and random with only dream logic. There were cases of witches who cast spells while sleeping, especially if they were having nightmares. The spells such witches cast were usually protective. They might cast a protective globe around the sleeping area. So Wren being unable to unlock the door himself was probably likely.

"Is there anyone else who might be able to open the door?" Maybe he had a second-in-command, or maybe the apprentices he brought in could dispel the magic.

"The spell itself is not a strong spell, but few people know that I lock myself in."

Something in Wren's expression caught her attention. Did he look guilty? Or maybe ashamed? If he was ashamed of the fact that he was not able to control himself, then he might not have told anyone. Or maybe he only told his trusted advisors.

"So, who knows?"

Wren sighed. "You."

Her gaze snapped to his face. Could she be the only one he had told? She only knew because she'd caught him in the act of sleepwalking. If he hadn't told anyone, how would someone know that the lock was on the door? They would know if they were trying to enter his room.

The thoughts worried her because there were very few reasons to try to get into someone's room without them knowing. He could have a lover.

"Do you have a special friend?"

Wren scrunched his nose, tilted his head, and then widened his eyes. "No one special. No one should be in my room."

"So the only way someone would know about the spell is if someone..." She didn't end the sentence because she didn't like the implication.

"Is trying to break in?" Wren asked her.

She shrugged. If no one knew about the spell, then the most obvious way to find the spell was to try to get into his room while he was sleeping.

He shook out his arms and shook his head. The emotions that flashed across his face were not something she had seen before. The mix of anger, regret, sadness, yearning and more expressions she could not decode probably meant he was too tired to think.

"Do you think it is related to the prophecy?" Wren asked.

Valeria snapped back from her thoughts. "What do you mean?"

"My sister told me that she had to leave for a while. I would not be able to see her until our birthday. That the world depended upon us."

Isolate the pair until first light on her day of birth

Seek the kept flame and release

Two halves united shall burn and be reborn.

The next line made no sense, but could Wren and his sister be the two halves? But why?

"You let her go?"

"My best friend swore to protect her." He slumped back into his bed, and he rubbed his eyes. "Even from me."

His words drew her sympathy. She knew what it was like to be away from her sister. How much harder would things be if her sister thought she needed protection from Valeria. "Then we need to make sure you are not able to sneak away at night."

"How?"

"I'll stay on the couch and put up a ward."

Wren must be exhausted because he didn't argue, and he started snoring when he shut his eyes.

Valeria stared at the ceiling wondering what was really going on. It took far longer for her to sleep.

9

———

WREN

<u>Morning, Primum second, 300 years post-Merge</u>

Later that morning...

Wren paced what he now called the phoenix room. Something had to change. The urge to see his sister was even worse this morning. Valeria sat at the table with his grandmother's journal opened. Removing his fire could be the key he needed to break the cycle. He sat on the chair opposite Valeria.

"We should cast the spell on me today."

He shivered at the skepticism in Valeria's expression.

"The line 'Seek the kept flame and release' from the prophecy could be me and the fire within." Wren held out a finger to count off his point.

"Or the line could refer to you opening the door with your fire." Valeria's voice was mild, but she seemed slightly worried.

"True." He sighed and rubbed his eyes. "I need to do something. You can't keep protecting me from sleepwalking from my couch."

"I don't mind."

"Someone broke into my room, which allowed me to leave the room with me not in full control. That puts you, me, and my Rookery at risk."

Valeria tilted her head. "The two might not be related. Someone opening your door the same night you sleepwalked might be a coincidence."

"Do you believe that?"

"No. Somehow the two are linked. We could set a trap for the person and catch them."

"We could." She needed to know the truth. "The urge to see my sister is getting harder and harder to resist even during the day. I need to do something, or I may end up as the next line: Two *halves united shall burn and be reborn*."

"Why would you and Alesia be two halves?"

"The burn part fits. My grandmother died by fire and so did my grand-uncle. I opened the door to this chamber with fire." He still didn't understand what the "half" part meant.

"Since you call this the phoenix chamber and there is a pattern of fire in your history you think that if you see your sister you will what? Spontaneously combust?"

Wren rubbed his neck and pushed down his feathers. He was not in control of his fire. The magic had just leapt up at the door. How could he say what would happen when he finally got to see his sister? "Maybe. I just know I have to try to fix this. If I lost my fire by the spell, that could make Alesia safe."

"So you think finding the spell was a sign."

Wren wrinkled his nose. Signs were soft things that could be interpreted many different ways. "When I went with my gut, I was able to open this chamber. The spell is worth a try. The sooner we do this, the sooner I can get you the protection charms."

The quirk of Valeria's brow said she was not fully onboard. She ran her finger down the text. "The spell says we need Frozen Birdsong. I don't know of anyone who has any."

"I have a small bottle in my office under lock and key." Wren knew what rare ingredients he had safely held in his office.

She grimaced and then nodded. "I need some things from my bag."

"I'll get the Frozen Birdsong and meet you back here in a few minutes." As Wren walked out of the phoenix room and down to his office, he wondered about his sister. This was dangerous. He needed to make sure if something happened to him, she would be taken care of. Alesia had refused to see him no matter how hard he'd tried. Walter had helped keep her away. Even though Walter was acting on Wren's request, he still could feel the anger bubble in his gut. Anger aside, he needed to send a note to his sister.

He strode to his desk and grabbed some paper. The note would go to Walter. "I may have a way to break the curse. If anything goes wrong, look after my sister. I'm sorry we fought. I love you both." How overly sappy but true.

He sighed and tucked the note in an envelope and pressed his stamp into the hot wax seal. A small flash of magic into the seal guaranteed that only Walter could open the letter.

His wooden delivery device sat on the bottom half of his window. Both ends of the long wooden box opened between the room and outside, but the inside was divided internally into twenty long slots. Wren had painted different colors inside each slot. Wren tucked the letter into Walter's bright green slot. A bird on the other side would grab the letter and deliver it for treats. Walter's slot got a lot of traffic, so the birds would be fast at delivery.

Wren strode back to his desk and unlocked his case. The contents in this cabinet were irreplaceable. He lifted the clear vial of Frozen Birdsong and swirled the magical component. The liquid sparkled as it flowed around the glass. The little vial had perhaps a tablespoon of the precious fluid. He'd never seen nor heard of another stash of Frozen Birdsong. If there was anyone else who had some, they were not saying. This very well could be his only chance to use this spell.

Wren walked back to the phoenix room.

Valeria bent near the lines of the spell circle. She traced the circle and the protective rune with her finger as if checking their integrity. She frowned and glanced up at him. Her brow pinched with what he thought was concern.

"It will be fine." Wren brushed the feeling that something was just not right aside.

"Have you ever just had a feeling about something you were about to do..." She grimaced and looked away.

Wren understood, but this was the only lead he had found on how to save his sister. "We need to take action. Removing my fire is the next thing to try. If we can get past our thirtieth birthday, the curse should be lifted." He knew this was dangerous, but if he didn't do something, Alesia would suffer the fate of his grandmother.

Wren sat cross-legged in the spell circle. The oddness of being in the middle paused him. He was rarely in the center of a circle as most of the time he was the one administering aid.

"The spell needed a place to put the fire." Valeria gestured at the twelve large, red, unlit candles that stood on the outside line of the circle.

"And those?" Wren pointed at the other dozen candles farther back.

"In case it gets too hot." She grinned at him, once again showing her mischievous side.

Warmth filled his chest.

"We will get this figured out," Valeria said as she continued to set up the spell. Despite being a witch, she checked everything on the spell circle. She was not sloppy or negligent but was funny and playful.

"You ready?" She sat on the cushion just outside of the circle.

His stomach twisted, but he nodded.

Valeria opened the bottle of Frozen Birdsong and sprinkled the contents of the vial between them. The sparkling liquid hovered frozen in the air. She closed her eyes. The feel of the magic changed in the room, and the spell circle snapped shut.

He relaxed his hands, which had fisted on his legs. Lowering his magical defenses took concentration. Valeria sang a song he didn't understand, which seemed to make the room blur. One drop of the Frozen Birdsong dissipated, leaving the scent of lavender.

A tickle and a tug pulled up faint heat from his chest. A sharp pain had him taking another deep breath and closing his eyes. Why did the flames hurt to remove? He sought the answer inside, but his thoughts felt heavy and fuzzy. Distant.

He'd pictured that the fire was in a separate place from his body. Even after opening the phoenix room's door, he hadn't sensed the fire.

He opened his eyes and engaged his mage senses. The image wobbled of Valeria pulling a bit of fire from his chest. Wrapped around the next bit of fire was something a lighter red or dark pink. As the flame pulled away from him, the pink something thinned and then broke. Pain hit his chest as the strand broke.

He brought his hand to his chest. The room shimmered, and his arm fell to his leg. The stone ground didn't look comfortable, but he really wanted to lie down. His eyelids grew heavier, making him aware of each blink.

Was the fire hooked into his soul? If the flame connected to his soul, then pulling the fire out might kill him. The question was, would taking that chance keep Alesia and his family safe?

Valeria tensed as if she felt that something was off but continued singing. The scent of lavender floated in the air.

She pulled another bit of flame and lit a candle. The room's temperature rose, causing sweat to bead on her forehead. A drop rolled down her face. She shivered but didn't stop the spell. Wren knew that she would stop if he said anything. He closed his eyes. If this was what he had to do to save his sister, then he would. He braced himself for the next bite of pain.

A door slammed open.

"Blackie, no!" Rye called out from the hallway.

He opened his eyes in time to see the black dog racing into the room. The dog lunged at Valeria, knocking her into the lines of the spell circle. The flame that had been stretching from his body snapped back. The Frozen Birdsong disappeared in a puff of lavender.

The backlash of the broken spell hit him in the chest, and everything went dark.

10

VALERIA

<u>Morning, Primum second, 300 years post-Merge</u>

The weight of what was probably Blackie moved on top of Valeria. She tried to push him off, but he wiggled closer. The charm Valeria had given Rye tinkled on his collar.

"I am sorry. I'm so sorry," the distraught young girl kept saying.

Valeria pushed the dog off enough to sit up. The dog came around and licked her face, leaving a warm wet trail on her cheek. He must be happy to see her.

Valeria scratched his nose and then pushed him away. The dog had broken the spell and the spell circle. The backlash blinded her magical senses. They should come back within a few minutes. Most of the candles lay scattered across the floor. Only the few with flames still stood. The Frozen Birdsong caught within the spell was gone. Wren lay unmoving on his side.

Her heart skipped a beat. She scrambled closer and rolled him over. His chest rose and fell, even if his face was paler than anything she had seen. She took a shuddery breath. The back-lash should have just blinded his senses. Why was he so affected? Unless the cause had something to do with the candles that still had flames?

She wouldn't know how to help unless she knew what was wrong. She stood and approached the candles still with flames. The flames flickered with something more than just fire.

Her stomach twisted as fear rose. Had the spell actually ripped off parts of Wren's soul? Why would he have allowed that? Even as she thought that, she knew the answer. Wren would sacrifice himself for his family without hesitation.

Rye touched Valeria's shoulder, startling her.

"Are you okay?" Rye asked.

Valeria nodded. Her mind whirled with ideas on how to help Wren. Could the soul damage be related to Wren being knocked out? Was there anything Valeria could do?

Valeria meant to glance at the girl but instead stared. Meeting Rye last night in the hall, Valeria had not had a chance to see Rye in the full light of day. The girl must be a recent addition to the tower. She was too thin and her cheekbones almost cut through her face, but her skin had the healthy glow of someone who had been eating well recently. Oddly, her eyes were still shadowed. Valeria bit her lip to keep from asking who was hurting Rye. Valeria had made a promise, and until she had an idea who was behind the unhappiness she saw in Rye, Valeria would stay quiet.

Rye did have the faintest glow of magic. Her magic naturally drew things together. The girl might be able to help with restoring Wren's soul, but Blackie would have to be kept away.

"Where is Blackie?"

Rye sighed and rubbed her eyes. "He ran away."

"Close the door. I want you to help me with Wren. Willing?" Valeria watched Rye carefully. If the girl was hesitant, that could interfere with Valeria's spell.

Rye blinked and she grinned. She looked eager to help, and there was no sign of fear.

Valeria's magical senses slowly recovered, and the soul pieces in the flames became obvious. With Rye helping perhaps a simple stitching spell would work. Wren was not awake to fight her, and there was only so long before returning them would be impossible. He would be stronger with his soul pieces back.

Casting a fire charm to keep herself safe, she transferred the flames to her finger. Adding back the flame would go better if she added them one at a time. They still would not reconnect without magical help.

"What are you doing?" The girl's voice sounded awed.

"I'll need you to help soon."

"How does the flame not hurt you? I can see a glow in the fire. What are—"

Valeria laughed. "Slow down and watch what I do. Actually, you can connect to my magic and see what I am doing. Touch my arm."

Rye shimmied in place and then put her hand on Valeria's arm. A shiver traveled up her shoulder. Rye had a strange feel to her magic, but the magical signature was so faint, Valeria had a hard time identifying why. The feeling wasn't bad, just strange. Valeria closed her eyes and let Rye see the magic.

"Oh, it is beautiful," Rye whispered, and she touched Valeria with her other hand. "What do I do?"

Rye's touch raised the hairs on Valeria's arms.

"Think about his soul reconnecting." Valeria thought simple instructions would be best.

Valeria touched Wren's chest with the pad of her fingers and gently tapped into Rye's natural talent. The charm to fix small things rolled off her tongue. Her finger tingled, and the soul piece merged into his chest.

She waited a moment to see if there were any issues. Wren continued to breathe normally. Some more color flushed his face.

Valeria grabbed the remaining flames one at a time until she had returned them all.

"Will he be okay?" The sheen of tears filled Rye's eyes.

"You probably saved his life." Wren would have died if the spell had continued. The fact that the fire contained pieces of his soul was not visible within the spell she'd cast. By the time she would have been able to notice, it would have been too late.

Rye bit her lip but nodded. "I don't have much magic. Wren took me in anyway. I have not fit in very well because all I can do is link things together. And..." Her face reddened and she looked away.

Valeria debated about asking who was hurting Rye again. They were alone, but the desperate plea to not talk about the issue held Valeria back. "Linking things can be useful."

Rye sighed. "Not when the ingredients mash together and can't be separated."

"You helped me put back Wren's soul. Not many others could help with that. You just have to be creative about how you apply your magic."

"I guess." Rye glanced around the room. "What were you trying to do?"

Valeria hummed and then patted Rye's shoulder. "Remove the fire from Wren. We had no idea that the fire was embedded in his soul."

Rye reached out toward Wren, but Valeria stopped her.

"We shouldn't touch him yet. I am watching his aura to see when we can." Wren's aura still looked odd, and she didn't want to chance that moving him would somehow wreck what they had tried to fix.

Rye nodded. "How do we take the fire out of Wren without hurting his soul?"

"I'm not sure it is wise to try again."

"But what if we did?"

Since the fire was mixed in his soul, the only thing that might help would be the spirit plane. That wouldn't be wise. Wren probably couldn't do magic there, and if anything went wrong, it would be far too easy to die. "We might need to bring him to the spirit realm to do so."

"What's that?"

"It's the place that overlaps with this world that the souls of the dead pass through before they go to the beyond."

"What's beyond?"

"Not sure. But I have been to the spirit realm. Witches can access the realm. The act brings us closer to the Goddess and earth magic."

"What about mages?"

"We would have to ask Wren. But I have only ever seen dying creatures with souls and a few other witches." Wren could speak to Rye about mage magic.

"What's it like?"

"The spirit plane can be a lot like here, except space and time do not work the same. I am able to fly through that world and even see back into this one."

"What about demons?" What was Rye's fascination with demons? Valeria had no idea what Rye's background was. Perhaps demons had made her an orphan? Perhaps they had more in common than Valeria had first thought.

"I have seen demons there." Alex made her realize that the spirit realm must also overlap other realms, not just this merged world.

"So can you die in the spirit world?"

"Yes. And you can kill demons there." Valeria shuddered remembering her own fight with the demon who had been joined to her soul. Only by entrapping the demon and compressing the magic did the demon die.

"You killed a demon?" Rye's voice rose in surprise and her eyes opened wide. "How did—"

Wren cleared his throat. "What happened?" He blinked slowly and seemed dazed.

"The spell was interrupted." Valeria sat next to Wren. She resisted the urge to take his hand.

He closed his eyes again. "Do we have any Frozen Birdsong left?"

"No."

Wren sighed and slumped.

"Wren, I have a message for you. That's why we were up here." Rye took out an envelope from her pocket and handed the envelope to Wren.

He opened the message and read the piece of paper within. Wren paled. If Valeria hadn't been watching him so carefully, she wouldn't have noticed the flash of black in his aura. Unease twisted her stomach. She must be seeing things after the intense spell.

"What's wrong?" Rye asked.

"It's a response back from my sister." He cleared his throat and read, "Malevolence cloaked in innocence draws us together. Its victory will be our failure."

Wren crushed the note. He stood and without another word, left the room.

11

WREN

Wren took another sip of the honeyed liquor. The liquid burned down his throat. The shelf dug into his side, but he didn't care. He deserved the pain. His sister wanted nothing to do with him. The urge to see her burned in his chest. For some reason, the alcohol made that urge easier to resist. The message from his sister crackled in his hand. His sister hated him, and she was going to die because he failed.

He took another sip. There was something wrong with him. The booze didn't stop the ache in his chest or the twisting feeling of failure, but the buzz made him care less. He just wanted everything to go away for a while. That was why he was on the top shelf of his library, so that no one would know where he was.

A click drew his attention, and a small trickle of magic from the alarm spell on his library door flared along his nerves.

Voices seemed to come from far away. A man and a woman? Were they in his head? Maybe. He'd had a lot to drink. He hiccupped.

"You like books." Wren recognized Serene's voice.

Footsteps drew closer to his location.

"Each one holds a promise of something new. A distillation of a story or of knowledge," the man whispered.

People moved directly below him. He scooted to the end of the shelf so he could look down. A dark-haired man with pale skin stood next to a slender woman with long, dark hair.

"Where is he?" Serene glanced around and then paced forward and touched the end shelf.

The man glanced around and then up. His green eyes widened when he met Wren's gaze. Wren had no idea who this was. He did not disappear when Wren blinked. Maybe the human was real.

Serene followed his gaze. "Blazes. He's drunk."

Wren leaned forward to make sure they were really real. The bottle slipped from his hand and crashed to the floor, shattering. The glass sparkled on the floor. Was the sparkle due to magic? Serene and the man might be real. He should ask.

"What are you doing here?" Wren's voice slurred.

"We need your help," Serene said.

"Why would I help you?" Wren hadn't disliked Serene. She was just another in a long line of projects his sister took on. Besides, he hadn't been able to help anyone today. His chest ached.

Seek the kept flame and release

He'd failed to release his flames. How would they fulfill the prophecy? His sister was still going to die.

"Then help Max." Serene gestured to the human next to her. The way her expression stayed closed, he realized she must think he hated her. He'd already messed things up today. He was better off not trying to help. He hiccupped.

"No." Wren turned away.

"I lost both my sister and brother. Your sister is alive." The emotion in Max's voice had Wren flinching. She was for now, but he had failed her.

"Mine isn't. I would give anything to have my little sister back," Max said.

His words punched Wren's chest and squeezed his heart. He wanted to see his sister so badly. She didn't want that. Wren turned and stared at Max with wide eyes.

"There was nothing I could do to save her, and she died in my arms." Max's voice rose and shook at the end. "Alesia is still alive. Do you know what that means?"

Wren shook his head. Thoughts and feelings swirled, almost making him dizzy. There was something definitely wrong with him.

"It means you still have a chance to make it right." Max stared into Wren's eyes.

Wren looked away and closed his eyes. Max was correct. He still had a chance. Alesia's birthday was still two days away. Maybe there was an action he could take. Even if she didn't want to see him. Pain radiated up his chest.

"He needs a bath and some food. Maybe some tea or something. Can you help get him something to eat and drink?" Emotions Wren couldn't interpret flashed across Max's face.

Serene nodded. "I'll have the servants draw him a bath and get food."

"Take your time." Max watched Serene walk away and then turned his gaze to Wren.

The sound of Serene walking away wasn't loud. The click and the flush of magic on the door said she had left them here.

"Did you want me to help you down?" Max asked.

Wren flinched and looked down at Max. Wren was an Aero. How would some humans help him? "As if you, weak human, could."

Wren blinked and then Max was up next to Wren. Max grabbed the harness straps and tugged. The harness jerked, and Wren shifted toward the edge. Max wasn't going to be able to do anything. The smug satisfaction had just settled when Max jumped back from the shelf dragging Wren with him.

The world tilted, but Wren didn't hit the floor. No, Max held Wren bridal-style. Before Wren could say anything, Max carried Wren across the room and dumped him in a chair.

Wren gaped at Max and clutched the straps. No human should be that strong.

Max walked away and came back with a glass of water. "When my sister died, I went on a bender. I drank all the booze in the house. I was a mess. All I could think of was that it was my fault she'd died."

Wren shuddered. He was doing the same, and Alesia was still alive. The push and pull of his emotions held him ridged.

Max held out the glass to Wren.

"The truth was, it was her choice. She felt called to help the sick of the town. And she did until she caught the sickness and died. I went to her then. For her, I would brave the risk of getting sick." Sorrow filled Max's expression. The set of the jaw said maybe he hadn't accepted that it was her choice.

"What's your point?" Wren took the offered glass and sipped.

"Your sister has made a choice you don't agree with. She hasn't died from it."

"Yet," Wren ground out, sounding stubborn and yet protective, even to his own ears.

"Wouldn't you rather be there to help her when she needs it?"

Wren grumbled and closed his mouth, not wanting the

words to escape. Not wanting Max to know Alesia didn't want his help. The thought stabbed his chest. He wanted to scream.

"What?"

"Human, you don't understand."

"Is your sister dead to you right now? Did her choice make you never want to forgive her?" Max stared at him as he asked.

"No." Wren snapped his mouth shut after that single word. The anger, regret, and sadness fused, leaving his chest a heavy mess. Why was he so emotional?

"Then quit acting like she's dead. She's not."

Wren's head snapped back as if Max had struck him.

No, his sister wasn't dead, but she would have nothing to do with him right now. Every attempt to communicate was rebuffed. It was almost like she no longer cared. The idea sent a stab into his chest. Logically he knew it wasn't true, but his emotions were in a turmoil over the possibility. Did she finally grow to hate him for the curse she set upon herself that day in the fortune teller's place? Wren slumped into the chair.

A furtive movement on the bottom shelf caught his attention. A dark snout pointed out from between some books. Blackie's gaze met Wren's, and the dog gave a big dog-smile. The damn dog was going to get hair all over the books. He didn't have the energy to care.

A few minutes later, Serene came back into the room trailed by two of Wren's people.

"The bath is ready." Serene glanced between the two men and then pressed her lips together.

His two personal guards came into the room. Wren ignored their strange expressions as he let them help him to his room.

He focused on tapping into the spell that allowed him to eavesdrop on anyone in his library. The room wavered, but he managed to get the spell in place, one which would burn off the alcohol more quickly.

His door opened, and Rye stuck her head in. "Hi, Wren." She glanced around the room.

"Rye?"

"Wren, I have to tell you something." Her voice lowered, and she took a step closer.

Wren tried to not huff. The girl was a menace with her dog. "Is it about Blackie?"

"Yes." Her voice got even quieter. "We need to talk about Blackie." Her gaze darted behind him, and she flinched away.

"You wanted to tell me where the dog was? That he had gotten into the library?"

Her face paled. "Yes. He didn't mean it. He just likes being by you."

The dog in question trotted up and rubbed against Rye.

She looked up at Wren with sad, almost tearful eyes.

He sighed. "It's fine. Just try to keep a better track of him."

"Yes, Wren. I'll try." She turned and left. The dog trotted after her.

He finished cleaning up and then through the spell he heard, "Wren and Walter were best friends. Alesia left the tower to be with Walter," Serene said.

In the silence, Wren could almost hear Max thinking. "Why?"

"Walter is part of the lizard-folk." In the time that Serene had spent at the Rookery, she had always been reserved. Their relationship had started with Serene being key to Alesia's rescue. Serene had only opened up to Alesia. In fact, Serene had become one of Alesia's best friends.

He knew she thought he hated her. He didn't. He didn't care that she was a shifter or that she had been hunted by the Human Protection Agency when they had first met. Alesia had petitioned hard for Serene to stay. He would have let Serene stay without his sister's support. He had looked into Serene's haunted eyes and had not been able to send her away. Especially after rescuing his sister.

Wren used more magic to clean himself and slipped into new clothing. Max was right. Not that Wren would tell him that. Even if his sister was angry with him and did not want to see him, she was still alive. Wren still had a chance to save her.

Serene chuckled sadly. "She's also a princess."

"So, she gets an arranged marriage?" This time Max's answer was quicker and a little more tart.

"Oh no, she can choose her mate."

The spell caught Max's quiet huff. Wren fixed his last button and hurried back toward the library.

"Then what's the problem?" Max asked.

Serene sighed. "Alesia is special and very important to her people. I don't know much, but it has to do with her grandmother."

Mention of his grandmother made fury roll up Wren's chest. He slammed the door open. Max jumped to face him. His expression flickered between shock and fear.

"It's my sister you are talking about." Wren's voice came out a snarl. Why was he so irrational?

Max took a breath and straightened his shoulders. "So you don't trust the guy?" Max asked.

"I trust Walter with my life." Wren stormed deeper into the room. He would not have allowed Alesia to stay with anyone else.

Max took half a step away before he lifted his chin and straightened his spine.

"Wren is very protective of his sister." Serene made calming motions with her hands, which did nothing to calm the rage within Wren.

"It sounds like he doesn't want her to be happy," Max said softly. If his spell wasn't still in effect, Wren never would have heard him. Max's words sent another wave of anger through Wren's chest. He whipped out his long sword.

Max's face twisted in fear, but he didn't back down.

Serene took half a step back and reached to grab Max. "We'll leave." Her voice was low and soothing but still did nothing to un-ruffle his feathers.

Wren couldn't read the emotion that crossed Max's features. Resignation? Regret? "After this is all over, if you want to have a duel to the death, I'm in. Right now, I have to do my duty to my people. You should understand that."

Grudging admiration warmed Wren's chest and pushed some of the anger away. Max may be a jerk, but he understood as few did about the weight of responsibility to one's people. Wren breathed in and out for a full minute. He worked to release his anger. His crest slowly lowered. "I'll hold you to that." Another minute passed, and Wren put the sword back into its sheath.

Max let out a relieved breath.

"What do you need?" Wren asked.

"We need you to magically restore Max's memories," Serene said.

If the cause of the memory loss was an active spell, Wren might have a chance. Otherwise, the human mind was too complex for his magic to be much good. Wren flipped to his mage sight. Max's aura seemed clean with no active spells in effect. There were no suppression spells or other restrictive spells. The spell could be hidden.

"Tell me what's going on first."

Serene stepped forward. "Max and Rose are from the town of Hope, which is located near New Nadezhda. During the Merge the wizards in town put up a shield to protect them. Now, the people inside are dying as are the crops. Both Max and Rose were sent to find special stones that were supposed to be able to save the town."

A guard came in and handed Wren a piece of paper.

"Max has no memories of what happened since he crossed the shield five years ago. We need to find out what is going on to save the town of Hope."

Wren glanced at the words on the sheet. He didn't see them. He listened intently to what Serene was saying. The story seemed fantastical. He was at a dead-end with his sister's issues. Even if there were only days until their thirtieth birthday, maybe helping Max and Serene would aid him in some way. At the very least, Alesia still loved Serene like a sister. Assisting Serene was the right thing to do.

"We found Max in a crypt being pumped full of terrible things."

Maybe the memories were lost because of what they had given him and not through a spell. Wren didn't know how to restore his memories, but maybe Valeria did. He thought about the Meeps encounter. Witches, at least his witch, seemed to have a whole world of magic open to them. He slowly sank into the chair behind his desk. Should he introduce Max and Serene to Valeria?

Serene stopped talking. Wren debated about starting the conversation, but where did he start? He shuffled papers. Even though he had magically purged the alcohol from his system, he still could feel the grouchiness and anger as if he were hung over. Everything felt hard, which was dumb. He was one of the strongest mages in the city. He had no reason for him to feel this way. His earlier anger still simmered.

Serene glanced at Max. Her lips were pulled into a grim line. Was she expecting him to say something, or was she disappointed that Wren wasn't responding? Confused impulses rushed through him. He both wanted to and didn't want to help.

He had his own issues to deal with. Did he really need the distraction?

Max sighed. "We can fight now."

"No. You both agreed to delay." Serene took half a step closer to Max. She must be feeling protective of him.

"He's only going to give us half-assed answers. He's not actually going to help us solve the problem. He probably even realized something. What we want is not going to aid us, or he has some other piece of information that changes the picture drastically. And then he'll do exactly as we ask of him and will giggle inside that he tricked us."

Wren stood. He didn't know anything but that Valeria might be able to help. "I don't giggle."

Max sagged. "You do know something."

Wren drew his sword and tilted his head. He didn't really. He only knew he couldn't help Max. Not the way he wanted Wren to. A magical cure for his loss of memories was probably impossible. The anger heated his chest. Max put him in this impossible situation of failing again. "I think I do."

Max bit back a curse.

Wren took a small breath to calm his rage. Such emotion was not like him. He felt like something fed his emotions, making him more volatile. To distract himself, he focused on a bag on the floor behind Max. The heavy burlap sack was used to bring goods into the Rookery. Such bags were easier for the flying folks to carry. The bag should not be on this level. Just like Max should not be here. Wren kept his mouth shut because he was not sure what he would say.

Serene made a frustrated huff.

"How about we make some kind of trade?" Max asked evenly.

"Saving all the people you love must be worth a lot," Wren said blandly.

"It is." Max lifted his head, resignation and perhaps some

dread pulled at his mouth. "But I think it's the same as how you value your sister."

Wren hesitated. He just wanted to go curl up in his nest and contemplate how badly things were with his sister. The thought sent a stab of pain through his chest. "What did you have in mind?"

"I can be your intermediary."

Wren raised his brows. Max's offer was audaciously brazen. He had no real contacts besides Serene and no reputation. "You think I would trust you for that?"

"Yes, because I can be trusted. When my issue is cleared up, I'll come and help you any way I can." Max winced. His words put him at Wren's mercy.

"You are a terrible negotiator," Serene muttered and threw herself back into Wren's chair. "Why don't you guys sit?"

"I am not going to put my people at risk to make a better deal." Max's tone left no doubt that he thought he was sacrificing himself for his people.

That left Wren standing. He walked stiff-legged to a chair but didn't sit down.

"You remind me of Alesia." Wren put his hand on the back of the chair. "I can't help you with your memories, but I have someone visiting from the Southern District who can give you what you need." The Southern District was where many witches came from. As far as he knew, Valeria had never lived there. Saying that was better than admitting that he and Valeria had just met.

"Thank you," Max said.

Wren nodded. He could do this. Introduce them and then assist Serene in some way.

"Who is here? Are you having a council meeting?" Serene asked.

"That is her business." Wren was not going to disclose his own plans to them.

Serene's eyes narrowed, but she said nothing.

Wren led them down two flights of stairs. When they reached the bottom, Serene scooted close to Max and whispered. "If she's on this floor, she's either very powerful or a friend."

Wren knew he must be smiling by the shocked look on Serene's face. "Or both."

He had a legitimate reason to talk with Valeria. His chest warmed, and the day seemed brighter.

Wren led them down a hall to a plain wooden door. He brushed his hand across the front of his shirt and stood straighter. Then he knocked formally.

A moment later, Valeria opened the door. Her pale blue eyes glanced behind him. "Can I help you?"

"Valeria, may I introduce Max and Serene." At Serene's name, Valeria huffed. Did she know Serene? Valeria was friends with Alex, who was friends with Joshua, so maybe she did.

"May we come in?" Wren asked.

Valeria stepped back into the room. She glanced at Wren and then invited them in.

She'd been busy. He'd never seen a spell circle quite like the one in the middle of her floor. Two swirling circles made of gold lines looked like a wheel with spokes connecting the outside ring to an inner smaller ring. Six cushions rested in the outer ring's openings. The spell circle was probably designed for a specific reason.

"Please pick a cushion and sit," Valeria said.

Max hesitated and glanced at Serene.

Serene pursed her lips. "The last time I sat in a spell circle was because my son was trying to figure out if something was contagious. Why do I feel the same way now?"

Interesting. Wren was unaware that Serene had a son. Even though Max was not her son, she definitely was protective of him.

"You will have to humor Valeria. I vouch for her." Wren sat on the light blue cushion.

"I know she's trustworthy, or she wouldn't be in this tower. I'd like to know what she's looking for with this spell circle." Serene crossed her arms. The tilt of her chin communicated her stubbornness on this point.

"I am checking you for riders and other forms of possession. Please sit, and I will answer your questions," Valeria said.

Her words surprised Wren. He hadn't thought with her demon issue that every new acquaintance might be a pawn of the demons. Finding out if someone was possessed was not always easy, unless the demon was in full control. Demons and their influence could be hidden until activated.

"Do I need to be careful of the lines?" Serene asked.

"No need." Valeria went to a desk in the corner and picked up a bag and a candle. Then she sat on a brown cushion next to Wren. She set her bag in her lap and set the candle in an open space within reach of her cushion. Why had she set up the cushions? Did what they chose matter? As a mage such a choice would matter only if the cushion itself was a spell component.

Serene nodded and sat on the red cushion across from Wren.

That left Max the choice of a pink, a purple, or a gold cushion. He looked between them and wrinkled his nose. "May I remove the cushion and sit on the floor?"

Valeria nodded her permission. He chose the spot directly across from Valeria and next to Serene.

He still couldn't tell if the choice of location and cushions had any meaning to Valeria. Was that choice part of a test? He hadn't seen Valeria attempt any other spell but the one to remove his flames and bring the Meeps together. Her next step should be to add magical power and intent in the circle. Unlike his own circles, this one did not have her intent already laid within the lines.

Valeria pulled a silk-covered package out of her bag. She nodded and then closed her eyes. A small sparkle of magic flowed to the circle's lines. When she opened them again, her eyes glowed a faint green as she stared at Max. "I have never had an undead in my spell circle before."

Wren swiveled his head to glare at Max. Undead were evil minions of darkness. If not for Valeria's carefully constructed spell circle, he would destroy Max.

12

———

VALERIA

Valeria watched Max. He was fortunate that she had constructed this spell circle in her room. The design was deeply personal and allowed her to seek deeper answers. This was the spell circle that allowed her the first step in the journey to break free from her demon family.

The Goddess had brought Max here for a reason with this spell circle already constructed. That meant she needed to seek answers in this case and not jump to conclusions, even though he was an undead and she'd never run into one who was not, at the core, evil.

She wasn't sure what was going on. Through her use of either her normal or magical senses, Max didn't appear to be undead. It had taken him entering her spell circle for her to realize that fact. Had her family sent Max to try and kill her?

Instead of attacking her, he looked flummoxed with wide eyes and a dropped jaw. She sensed no ill intent. She activated her truth spell from her tattoos and embedded the magic into her circle.

"He doesn't know." Serene's voice was calm but strong. Her expression was kind and motherly.

Max swiveled to look at Serene, looking even more confused.

Valeria relaxed the spell she'd started when she'd realized what he was. She examined him with the magic of the circle. His spirit still resided in his body. The magic that held his spirit in place was not evil. In fact, if she was reading the magic correctly, the mix of protective and divination meant he was a guardian. A guardian of what she had no idea. As she watched him, a faint trail of black slithered across his aura and then hid. She shivered. The magic felt familiar, but she wasn't sure why. He probably had a rider, an evil spirit embedded in his soul, or some other mostly inactive magical spell.

"How is that possible?" Wren demanded.

"What are you talking about? I'm not undead." Max crossed his arms. He told the truth. Whatever was going on, he had no idea what was happening.

Valeria needed to help him determine what he was a guardian of. First she had to get him to accept his undead nature, find out what the sliver of evil was, and determine if she could remove the magic. "May I see your hand?"

Max hesitated. He made a fist and then very slowly extended it to her.

She gripped his hand firmly with his thumb and pinky. If he had masked his evil intent, when she cast the next spell, he would attempt to escape her hold. She closed her eyes and murmured the spell and allowed herself to feel the room. She was vulnerable like this, but taking this step would allow her to access her full power. The feeling of fragmentation assaulted her. "You have missing memories?"

"Yes, I guess I've been here five years. I only remember crossing over," Max said quietly.

She could sense the gaps from his missing memories, but the biggest pull was where he had been from. An image of a town sign with the word Hope appeared. "Would you say you are driven to save Hope?"

"Wouldn't you be?" Max blinked.

She could almost see his thoughts flicker across his consciousness. Lightning zapped across his aura, and he jerked just slightly. Whatever that thought was would help her determine what was going on. "What did you think there?" Valeria asked.

"A-about my wife, Eleanor." Max's whole body lit up. He loved his wife, and that love was connected to the evil. In fact, the evil might be using his love to shield its presence. She could only hope Eleanor was still alive.

Valeria nodded and closed her eyes. She murmured words that brought her magic to focus. The baking bread and tinkling bells led her deeper in her power.

She watched his thought process and got a feel for how hard it would be to remove the evil. This evil could be connected to his undead life. If she removed the magic, he might die. She had to tell him and let him decide how to proceed. She had one more test.

Valeria opened her eyes and turned her gaze to Max.

"What does it mean if I am undead? Will I turn into a zombie or a skeleton and attack the town? Am I a danger to others?" He worried his lip and kept his gaze on Valeria.

She revealed her tattoos. He should either be attracted to touch them or repelled, depending on his default alignment.

He jerked his arm back.

She gripped his hand tighter. The jerking away could have

meant anything. She needed to know if she could let him leave this spell circle. "Why did you jerk your hand away?"

Max's face flooded with color. "I want to trace the symbols. See how many you have. Touch each one."

He was a good man who had been converted to a special kind of undead guardian but probably had been turned by something evil that left a spell to control him. She hid her tattoos while she decided what to say. He would not take kindly to the evil within him. The evil itself might react to her revelation. "I have good news, strange news, and bad news." Valeria leaned back and released Max from her gaze.

"What's the good news?" Serene asked.

"Max is not evil," Valeria said.

"Even if he was an ass, I sensed he was trying to help me." Wren brushed the feathers on his neck absently, which gave the impression he was deep in thought.

"What does it mean 'not being evil?'" Serene asked.

"Evil is the ultimate of being self-centered. No one else matters. No one else's desires, wants, or needs matter. Anyone could be sacrificed for what the evil person desires." Valeria pulled another item from her bag and unwrapped it carefully. She kissed the gray and gold stone and placed it on a space next to her.

Max shivered. "What's the strange news?"

"You are undead but of a kind I've never encountered. Life is fueled by positive energy. It grows and connects. The undead are usually created from negative energy. It keeps a body in a state it is not meant to be in. Most undead seek life energy to feed the negative energy." She decided to leave the guardian part for a future conversation.

Valeria unwrapped another item from her bag, a blue, silk-covered button, kissed it, and placed it on another open space.

She ignored Max's nervousness, waiting for him to ask his questions.

"Then what am I?" he finally asked.

"You are undead, but your body is still being fueled by positive energy."

"How do you know?"

How did she make him believe? "The tattoos you saw are a blessing. They were made specifically to keep evil out. You were able to touch me with no pain. In fact, they drew you. Only positive energy can stand to be near my tattoos."

Max bit his lip and sat back. His gaze grew distant.

"What spell are you casting? I don't recognize the pattern," Wren asked.

"Keep watching and see if you can figure it out." Valeria unwrapped another object, which, this time, was a tangled ball of purple yarn, and placed it in the last open spot.

"I thought wizards needed to concentrate while casting a spell." Serene glanced at Max and then met Valeria's gaze.

"I'm not casting the spell now. I'm setting the spell up. Besides, I'm a witch, not a wizard." Wizards and mages were different words for a practitioner with the same relationship to magic. There were so many rumors and misconceptions in the world about how magic worked. Both witches and wizards had that same trouble.

"What's the difference between a witch and a wizard?" Serene asked.

"It's in how they approach spells." Because Serene's interest seemed genuine, Valeria had no issue explaining some of the differences. The ways people connected to magic defined the label the world used for them.

"A wizard holds the magic outside of his or her body. They use objects as carriers. Their emotions get in the way of spells.

It's about control and logic." She'd expected Wren to smirk. He didn't. In fact, he seemed thoughtful.

Valeria grinned. "Whereas witches have their magic inside. Both schools are about control. Witches use objects to evoke feelings that fuel the spell."

"A wizard isn't trained to use their emotions as fuel. If their emotions are involved, the spell will act in unexpected ways." Wren watched her as she pulled the remaining focus objects from her bag.

"And witches can't create spells for things they don't believe in. If they can't access their feelings or if they're lying to themselves, the magic won't work correctly, if it works at all." Valeria had her focus objects for a reason. They were more emotional components rather than spell components.

"So, the reputation of witches gaining power from devils isn't true?" Max asked.

Valeria paused and her gaze went to his. "For some witches that is true. The same way that only some undead are evil."

Max's flush almost made Valeria giggle.

She lit the candles within arm's length, which drew his gaze back to the swirl of lines on the floor. "Figured out what I'm doing?" Valeria purposely made her tone teasing.

"Not at all." Wren shook his head and looked frustrated. "Your spell components make no sense."

Valeria pointed to the tangled ball of purple yarn. "This has emotional meaning to me. I use it to seek the truth."

"Why yarn?" Wren asked. "I would have used something pure like salt or perhaps water."

"This yarn was with me when I went through my own truth finding. It has come to feel like the knots we tie ourselves into. The mix of truth and lies we all tell ourselves. It represents confusion."

"So, I would need to find objects with emotional meaning if I were to become a witch?" Wren asked.

Valeria raised her brow at Wren, and his mouth snapped shut. His face went red. Had he given up that she could help him, or was he just naturally curious?

"You still haven't told us the bad news," Serene pointed out.

"Just a moment." Valeria closed her eyes and stilled. Her movements became controlled. She focused inward on the core of her being. The scent of baked bread and the tinkling of bells heralded her power. A golden globe of magic appeared before Valeria.

She sent her intentions to the globe. The next step would require more protection. The golden ball shimmered and sank into the lines of the spell circle. The lines glowed and created a thin, golden barrier between them and the rest of the room.

Serene made a soft sound of surprise, but Valeria's gaze focused on Max, who looked at Serene. Would he accept her help?

"Nicely done." Wren looked at the shield and cocked his head back and forth.

"Max?" Valeria asked.

He shifted his fear-filled gaze to her.

"Will you let me help you?" Valeria asked. If he said no, then she wasn't sure what she would do. He'd be a danger to himself and those around him without help. Hopefully, he'd say yes.

"What will you do?" he whispered.

"Ask you questions and then reveal the truth to you."

"The bad thing?"

She nodded. "And then help you, if you want help with the bad thing."

He swallowed, and his face paled. After a long moment, he nodded.

She would ask an easy question first. "How do you feel about Hope?"

"I still need to save them. If I do, I can see Eleanor again." His face radiated his belief in that statement.

"How do you feel about Eleanor?"

He didn't answer, but the magic around him pulsed brightly. Valeria held his gaze, keeping him focused.

"How did you become undead?" Valeria asked.

"I don't know."

"I see the spell has a truth component to it," Wren said.

Max snarled. "Why don't you tell us why you and Alesia have a problem?"

Valeria lifted her hand. "Please. Before we fight, you must know there is some element of control on you. Something is driving you to seek Hope. It's using the energy of your feelings for Eleanor as a power source. Right now, it is goading you to fight."

Max stilled. "I don't understand."

"The control element might be what's holding you together as an undead. You may die if I break that bond."

She could see his panic, and the dark thread twisted around the golden glow. Did she know who cast the spell? Sometimes a mage or witch could sense the magical signature and if they knew the caster well, could even tell the person who cast the spell. This incantation seemed familiar.

Max gasped and shivered. His aura jumped and twisted. He closed his eyes. He took a slow breath. His aura stilled, the fear draining away, leaving determination. "Do you think removing the control element will kill me?"

"I have never seen an undead such as yourself, so I have no idea what might cause you to die."

"Beheadings and stakes to the heart are generally bad no

matter what energy animates your body." Wren's droll delivery almost made her laugh.

"That works on birds too," Max snarked back.

Wren smirked. "Why are you involved, Serene?"

"Joshua and I got word from Alesia to protect Rose," Serene said. "Alesia foresaw the need." She winced as if she hadn't intended to confess that fact to Wren. The truth spell affected everyone in the circle.

The rage that swept through Wren's aura was not a good sign.

13

———

WREN

<u>Afternoon, Primum second, 300 years post-Merge</u>

A mix of emotions rushed through Wren that he hadn't felt for a long time. His chest tightened, and his feathers twitched. His body was not able to decide if he was angry or sad, but anger seemed to be winning.

"You never told me that." Wren's crest rose and his neck feathers fluffed. Serene should have told him about Alesia's request to protect Rose.

"Remember how you said never to come back here again?" Serene asked sharply. She crossed her arms. Goddess, the woman had always been so stubborn. He could see how she and Joshua had become so close. They both were passionate martyrs.

"And yet here you are!" Wren growled.

Heat curled up his chest and down his arms.

"The control element is trying to get us to fight," Valeria said calmly.

Her words poked through the anger. She must be right. He rarely felt this out of control. "The spell is manipulating us?" Wren took a breath and opened his hands to release the negative energy. "Then removing the spell must be a good thing."

Serene looked at Wren. "I'm sorry I didn't tell you about Alesia. I hate seeing you two estranged. She misses you." Her voice was soft and every word she said felt sincere.

"I miss her as well. We can't be together until—"

"Hush, Wren, now is not the time. What is it you wish to do?" Valeria said. The last question was obviously spoken to Max.

Max stared at each person in turn. His face didn't give away what he was thinking. Wren could feel the magic currents twist around Max. The black and golden threads fighting for dominance. Valeria's powers fought to let Max decide his fate without the influence of the dark magic. Whatever magic had a hold of him was powerful, and the golden threads struggled.

"So, if I leave the spell alone, I may be a danger to my friends and family. If I attempt to have it removed, I might die?"

The golden magic must be winning if Max was able to say such a thing.

Valeria nodded. "The control element could force you to hurt your friends and family."

"Please, do it." Max's voice came out a harsh croak.

Valeria closed her eyes and swayed to some internal rhythm. She spoke in a low tone and lifted her hands, spreading her fingers wide. The golden energy thickened around them, blocking the rest of Valeria's room.

Wren could feel Valeria's magic surrounding them. Darkness hidden within Max seeped out from his core, like some kind of ooze. The darkness had not been there earlier. Wren gently added his own magical strength to Valeria. Instead of the hard slog to connect, their power meshed easily, almost with no extra effort, giving her the boost she needed.

Max hunched forward clutching his chest and cried out, sending a shudder through Wren. The sound reminded him of a funeral song to a mate. Max slowly slumped forward.

The black ooze formed a ball in the air. The golden energy wrapped around the sludge. Wren added more of his blue power, and the golden magic compressed the darkness. Wren focused and helped Valeria squish the blackness until the evil popped and disappeared.

The feeling of the room lifted. How powerful had that magic been to cast such a pall on the room?

Max opened his eyes and sat up. He blinked and glanced around as if he had just awoken.

"You lived," Valeria said, sounding relieved.

"You had me worried." Serene rushed over to help Max sit up.

"How do you feel?" Valeria asked.

"Much better. Much clearer." Max turned his attention to Valeria.

Wren could relate to the emotions on Max's face. He'd probably question everything that had happened and wonder if his choices were his or the spell's. Wren never wanted to be subject to such a control. He needed to be confident in his life and his choices and not have that extra worry.

"Why would I have a control element?" Max asked.

Valeria shrugged. "The fact you can ask that question now proves it's gone."

Something about her expression made Wren think she had seen something. "You have a guess?" Wren asked.

"Unless the control is to stop murderous impulses, such a thing is generally evil. It manipulates the person in complete disregard for what they want or how they feel. Max's control was about going back to Hope."

"To see my wife, I had to find the stones and bring Rose." The color drained from Max's face.

Valeria pursed her lips in thought. What the stones were was not important at this moment. "What about your missing memories?"

Max closed his eyes and his brow furrowed. "Not much, just gravestones and a sense of...pressure."

"You may remember with time." Valeria met Max's gaze. "A powerful mage cast the spell. An adept of the highest order. It was intricately and intimately constructed."

What was she hinting at?

"Meaning the person knew Max?" Serene asked, looking puzzled. She rubbed Max's back.

"Or had plenty of time to get to know him under duress." Valeria picked up each item from her spell circle, kissed the item, and wrapped them carefully before putting them away.

"I saw no indication he had been tortured." The wounds could have faded in five years.

"Manipulation is far easier than actual physical torture." Her voice was gentle and her gaze focused on Wren.

He grimaced. The Aeros did not subscribe to any sort of torture. Alesia's harrowing abduction by a faction within the Human Protection Agency had left him very aware that others did. The fact that Max had been tortured added a layer of sympathy toward Max. Things would be far easier in Wren's life if he could ignore that feeling. Serene had helped Alesia escape all those years ago. Without her help, Alesia might have died. No, she would have died. Between his sympathy for Max and the debt he owed Serene, Wren's only option was to continue to help Max. Helping was the right thing to do.

Max stood up and offered his hand to Serene. Usually, humans did that as a parting gesture. Now that Wren had decided to help, Max was not going to get rid of him easily.

"Where do you think you're going?" Wren asked.

"Back to Master Phil's. Rose and Joshua are meeting us there."

Wren frowned. "I'm going with you."

"What? Why?" Serene's startled face almost made him chuckle. He ignored the small ball of hurt her reaction gave him. He was not a monster. Failing to keep his loved ones safe didn't make him evil. His chest tightened.

"Alesia told you Rose should be protected. So, I'm going to help protect her." If they denied Wren, he would still follow them and find a way to give them aid. Things would be far easier if Max and Serene just accepted his assistance.

Serene's mouth opened and then she laughed a bit. "You would be a valued team member if you joined us." The sincerity in her voice soothed his hurt.

Max nodded. "Thank you."

Max's easy acceptance eased even more of Wren's worry. He could take the lead in finding out what was going on.

"I'll come as well," Valeria said.

Wren's plans fell apart with those words. Why would Valeria want to aid them? She didn't know these people. Did she? Wren glanced at Valeria and frowned. "I'm not sure that's a good idea."

Valeria seemed thoughtful. "It could help."

Wren flinched. She meant help with his own problems. His wings twitched. He wanted to fly away. His support hadn't been meant as an exchange of favors.

Wren stood abruptly, leaving Valeria's room. He needed to get a few things if he was going to aid Max. If this was what his sister wanted him to do, he would do what he could. Something still felt wrong, and he wished he knew where that feeling came from. Every time he tried to pin the feeling down, the urge to fly away gripped him.

"Are you okay?" Rye walked next to him down the hallway toward the stairs.

"Yes, we just have to go do something. Stay here." Wren flew up the stairs to his office. The last thing he needed was for poor, innocent Rye to get caught up with evil magic. She would have no way to defend herself if she were targeted. Or even worse, she would have to bring that darn dog. Who knew what mischief the dog might end up getting into.

Once he was done in his office, he flew down to meet the rest of his party. They walked together as a group away from the Rookery.

The closer Wren got to Shifterville, the more his mind whirled. He was missing something. The extra scenting announced the edge of Shifterville. For whatever reason, animals marking their territory remind him of Blackie. Wren hadn't caught the dog lifting his leg on anything yet, but Wren had found the dog in places he should not be. Maybe—

A high-pitched scream of anguish broke his musings. The scream sent a shiver down his spine. Max and Serene took off running toward the sound going through solid-seeming walls. Wren followed them deeper into Shifterville. Was that a human or some other creature screaming? He rounded the corner, and the scream started again.

The scream stopped abruptly. Never a good sign.

On the building up ahead was a closed door marked with a healer's sign. Max grabbed the handle, pulled, and ripped the door off its hinges, then tossed the door aside. Wren had his evidence that Max was not really a human. Max disappeared into the house. Valeria pushed her way inside, and Wren followed her.

A pale woman curled on the floor, covering her head. Her red ponytail wiped back and forth, and her body shook. She lifted her head, clenched her fists, and screamed as if she was being torn in half. It took him a moment to recognize Joshua's second-in-command, Rose. He couldn't see any obvious source of her pain until he engaged his mage senses. The same black miasma that had been around Max oozed around the woman. Joshua crouched near Rose, staring at Rose with his eyes wide. Whatever had happened to her must have happened quickly. Another shifter hovered in the background. He must be Master Phil, the healer they were going to.

"Break the necklace," Valeria ordered.

With her words, Wren focused through the miasma to the necklace's dark magic. The power in the necklace was subtle compared to the rest of the magic roiling around the woman.

Joshua lunged forward and pulled the necklace from around Rose's neck. The necklace chain broke in his hand.

Rose froze and then shuddered. The tension left her body, and she stood up in one slow motion. The room plunged even deeper into a sense of wrongness and evil. More dark ooze flowed out of Rose's skin and surrounded her aura.

Max reached out his hand and took a half step forward. "Rose?"

Rose turned toward the door, seemingly unaware of anything in the room.

Wren glanced at Valeria, who was pale and had bitten her lip. No one else in the room moved. They were not in a protective magical circle. The spell to catch and contain such darkness wasn't an easy one to do without preparation. Wren's own magical power was almost empty. Valeria was probably in the same state. Neither of them would be able to deal with Rose's issue.

This black ooze had fully shadowed Rose.

There were no good options.

Rose charged to the doorway. Max stepped in front of her, and she walloped him. Her fancy kick left Max sprawled on the floor. The darkness around Rose pulsed and reached toward Max. A flash of light pushed the miasma back. Rose grunted and turned to the gaping entrance. The fixed, vacant eyes stared on the exit behind Wren.

"Get out of her way!" Master Phil shouted.

Dark magic pulsed toward Wren as he dove to the side of the room.

14

WREN

Early evening, Primum second, 300 years post-Merge

The dark magic hissed past Wren and sent tingles down his arm. He landed hard on the stone floor, his shoulder twinging.

"Follow her," Master Phil said.

Footfalls rushed away before Wren could reorient.

When he looked up, Rose was gone. His stomach dropped. He leapt up and raced out the door. Even though he had little magic left, he needed to help protect her.

There had to be a way to contain the darkness within her. But first he had to find her. Perhaps he could use the signature of the dark magic to locate Rose. He spread his wings and flew to the top of the nearest house. The oddly shaped houses and twisty trails between them would make things more difficult but hopefully not impossible to track.

He closed his eyes and reached out for the evil that still should be nearby. That much darkness would leave a trace. He sensed nothing of that magnitude. Some thieves with evil intent skulked a few blocks away. Deep anger and fear hovered inside one of the nearby houses, but no true evil.

Frustration boiled in his chest, which only made his power dissipate. He pulled out his focus gem, took a calming breath, and concentrated on the way the magic had felt and what he knew about Rose. His magic scanned the area, seeking any clues about where Rose could be.

The gem slipped from his fingers, and he grabbed the crystal before it fell. He blinked his eyes open. Exhaustion weighted his shoulders down. How long had he searched? The sun hadn't set, so hours hadn't passed. It took him three attempts to get the gem back in its pouch.

Rose should not have been able to disappear like that. Not without the active interference of another powerful magic user.

Wren flapped down to the street and walked slowly back to the door. He'd failed Rose. His chest tightened, and his stomach twisted. More things to feel guilty about.

Nothing blocked the entrance. He stomped in to see a pale Valeria standing by Max, who still looked shaky on his feet. He'd gone down hard earlier.

Wren touched Valeria's arm. "Are you okay?"

She nodded, but he didn't believe her.

"I scanned the area. I wasn't able to track her. Something hid her from my magical senses." Wren shook his head. Should he mention his theory of two mages being involved? He would wait until he and Valeria were alone to compare notes.

Max cleared his throat. "Her scent is gone as well."

Hidden scent was another piece of the puzzle. At least two very powerful Mages must be behind Rose's afflictions. The situation could also be caused by strong mages with a large power source, which wasn't necessarily the same thing. By Valeria's foot shuffling, she seemed as uneasy as he felt.

Wren needed to move and think. The floor creaked under his feet as he walked back and forth. The pacing was not quite enough to break the deadlock in his head. The overwhelming pressure of failing lay heavy on his chest, making it hard to breathe.

"Can you help me fix this?" Max motioned to the door.

Wren nodded and helped him place the door back on its hinges. The odds that Rose or the mage who hid her would be back here were low, but why leave the house unprotected? Wren still had some power left, so the least he could do was repair the door. He could even add an alert so if anyone with evil intent entered Master Phil's home, Wren would know. He whispered a spell and embedded the magic in the door. The hinges grew together and grabbed onto the frame.

"Thank you," Max said.

Valeria sat cross-legged on the center of the floor in a chalk star etched around her, which meant she had an idea on what else she could try.

Max turned toward Valeria and opened his mouth to speak.

Wren made a shushing motion to stop him. Valeria's magic would work better if she was left to focus.

A moment later, Valeria sagged. "I also found no trace of her."

Wren blew out his breath. Valeria and he were two of the most powerful magic users in the city. Yes, they were both exhausted, but the fact that neither of them could track Rose was not a good indication that this would be resolved soon.

The door banged open and Joshua, Serene, and Master Phil stormed into the room.

"She's gone. What the hell is going on?" Joshua's red face and strident tone expressed how upset he was. Wren had never seen the man this emotional. But when Joshua's gaze landed on Wren, he realized no matter what their past rivalry had been or what nasty tricks they had played on each other, Joshua was here to help.

"Rose is under someone's control. I think it's the same person who had control of Max." Valeria's calm voice cut through the tension in the room.

Joshua took Serene's hand. He took a deep breath and closed his eyes for a moment before returning his gaze to Wren. "Tell me what happened, and I'll tell you about what Rose and I discovered."

Serene told them about what they'd discovered with Valeria in the spell circle. Wren noticed she didn't mention how Max knew Rose or of finding Wren drunk.

Joshua wrapped his arm around her and kissed the top of her head. "Did you know Rose was undead too?"

Wren froze. That made so much sense now. She had always been extraordinary. How had her undead status stayed hidden for so long? What did it mean if there were two undead who were not evil? Valeria had acted like she might know more. He would have to add that to the list of questions they talked about in private.

Serene smiled at Joshua. "It was not my secret to share."

"They are the same kind of undead." Master Phil added a pot to the fire. His hands shook as he did so, but he'd had a good idea to distract himself and help others. They would need food and planning to locate and aid Rose. "We can't track her in normal ways. She left behind no scent and is far faster than we are."

"She's also magically blocked from scrying," Wren added. Blocking his senses was very difficult. Wren lost track of the conversation as the exhaustion weighed him down.

"Max has no knowledge of how he became an undead. The truth circle would have forced him to reveal it." Valeria's voice snapped him back.

Max asked, his voice hesitant, "Do you think my memories could be restored?"

"Not by magic. They'll come back when you're ready." Valeria shook her head, but smiled at Max. The smile was soft and compassionate and made Wren's heart beat a little bit faster and added a sour twist to his gut. Could Valeria find Max attractive? Not that he cared or that this was the right time to be thinking such thoughts. His own derailed quest and the new one that Alesia supplied were not going well. He just must be very tired.

"Or not at all," Wren felt compelled to add. "What do Max and Rose share?"

"They have being from Hope in common." Serene tried to step away from Joshua.

"Maybe Hope is filled with the living dead. Maybe they were turned when they were protected from the Merge. A spell gone wrong." Joshua pulled her to his chest and nuzzled her ear. Serene's face reddened, and she huffed in what seemed like surprise. Why was Joshua being so overly affectionate to Serene? Wren reviewed every interaction he could remember with the stoic man and came up empty. Perhaps he was feeling his own mortality?

"Do undead have children?" Max asked.

"No?" Valeria said, not sounding certain at all.

Wren didn't know anything about Max but what he and Serene had disclosed. Both Rose and Max coming from Hope had something in common and perhaps explained how they got here. "Maybe leaving Hope and crossing the shield is what did it." Wren stared at Joshua, who continued to nuzzle Serene.

"Do we know if anyone else has come across the shield?" Master Phil must have been thinking similar things to Wren.

"I have no idea. No one went near the shield. Warnings were posted. But who knows?" Max fidgeted.

"No kids disappeared?" Master Phil pressed.

"When I was much younger, we did have a kid who we know went through the shield. All that was left was his clothing." Max nodded.

"Rose wasn't naked when she came through," Joshua said.

"How could you possibly know that?" Serene tried to step away from Joshua, but he pulled her closer. She gave an exasperated eye roll. The action flagged Wren's gut.

"I didn't know it at the time. But I met her right after she crossed over." Joshua had never been particularly demonstrative. The emotion didn't feel quite right because his jaw was too tight and his grip was just a bit too possessive.

"None of this is helping us find her. It was like she fled." Max glanced at the door.

Joshua snapped to attention with his arm still tucked around Serene. "Or like she was being called. She said she heard voices. They were calling her to come help them. To save them." So whatever was affecting Joshua was not interfering with his intellect.

Wren glanced at Valeria, who was also watching Joshua with a puzzled frown.

Max swallowed his Adam's apple bobbing. "I thought I heard something similar when we were fighting the zombies earlier in Shifterville."

Max and Serene had left out fighting zombies from their previous story. Did Wren need to upgrade the Rookery defenses?

"So the zombies and the voices could be related." Serene pushed Joshua's hand away. "Joshua, let go."

Was Wren imagining the interaction was odd? His gut said no.

"I just want to be near." Joshua fought to hold Serene close. "I think we need to go back to the cemetery."

"If we find her, what are we going to do? Carry her back?" Max crossed his arms.

"If I have to," Master Phil muttered.

Serene glanced at Joshua with a puzzled frown. "We need Valeria and Wren to break the spell. They did it once, so they can do it again."

Dark circles lay under Valeria's eyes, and her mouth pinched in a frown. She looked as tired as Wren felt. He would not be up to breaking such a spell now. Not without more mages or a power source.

"You can use my place if it would help." Master Phil gestured at the door. "I see you fixed the door."

"Sorry. I heard Rose screaming..." Max grimaced and ran his hand through his hair.

"We have another lead." Master Phil, too, turned to watch Serene slap Joshua's hands again.

Wren shivered and cast a quick spell to see the magic in the area. Viewing spells were things that apprentices learned and drew very little power. At first he saw nothing, but as he looked, a faint flash of darkness clouded his view of Joshua.

Had he been infected while he was searching for Rose? But why did he have overly possessive actions toward Serene? If he was not possessed, the magic must be coming from somewhere. He watched the pattern the magic wove and disappeared around Joshua.

"What lead?" Max asked.

"Rose was taking a potion from Glenn from the West District." Joshua's aura flashed the blackness again. The magic almost seemed as if the power was not quite in this world.

"Why is this a lead?" Max asked.

"She doesn't remember meeting him. He knew she was undead and was poisoning her." Joshua seemed unaware of how close he was standing to Serene.

"We can take the West Market." Serene pointed between herself and Master Phil.

"It's not safe. I should go with you." Joshua scowled and pulled her closer. A flash of black followed his words.

After living with Serene for so long, Wren could tell she was uneasy but didn't feel like she was in danger based on her small frown. "You know I'll be fine."

"Wren and I can stay here. We might need to create something more mobile for Rose." Rose was fast, strong, and compelled. A bad combination for getting her to walk into a spell circle and then hold still long enough to work the spell to free her. Valeria caught his gaze and widened her eyes. She tilted her head in a subtle question.

The pattern of magic seemed to be coming from something in Joshua's hand. Wren might need to distract Joshua. Wren nodded, barely moving his chin.

"Joshua, I think you and I should go to the cemetery," Max said.

Joshua pulled Serene closer and looked about to argue. His jaw was tight, and his eyes flashed with anger, but his face had paled and the faint tang of fear invaded the room. The black magic overshadowed his whole body. What the heck was going on?

"You see it?" Valeria asked Wren so softly he gave another slight nod and casually moved closer to Joshua. He knew Joshua better and could distract him away from what Valeria might need to do.

"What's going on, Lighthouse? You afraid?" Wren made sure to use a taunting tone and flung his arms out to catch his attention.

"What's your problem?" Joshua's eyes narrowed, but the magic didn't flare. Interesting. Whatever spell was affecting him, the magic seemed to be focused on Serene. Wren needed to be more dramatic.

"You." Wren stepped closer and pointed his finger at Joshua's chest.

Valeria lunged forward and snagged Joshua's hand. Wren grabbed his other arm, knocking Serene out of the way. Wren wrapped his arms around Joshua from behind. Joshua bucked hard. The dark magic flared, almost obscuring Joshua from Wren's sight. The scent of fear rolled off Joshua. The feel of wrongness permeated the air.

"Serene." Joshua sounded frantic. He bucked and twisted, but wasn't able to break Wren's hold. "Are you hurt?"

"Open your hand," Valeria demanded.

Joshua shook in Wren's arms. The black magic rolled off him in waves.

"Let me go! Serene needs me." Joshua fought Wren's hold, bucking and kicking. He acted nothing like the trained agent Wren knew him to be.

"Open your hand, and we'll let you go to Serene." Valeria's voice softened and had an edge of entreaty.

Joshua bucked one last time and then stilled.

He must have opened his hand because Valeria darted forward with a cloth wrapped around her hand. The black magic froze and shattered.

Joshua's whole body relaxed. He took a shuddery breath. "Thank you. I was deathly afraid of losing Serene."

Wren released Joshua and stepped back. Even with the spell gone, giving Joshua space was a wise action.

"Why did she run if the necklace was controlling her?" Max glanced nervously at Wren and Joshua.

"I think there may be two different people or factions who have opposite goals involved." Valeria tucked the necklace in her pouch. The pouch glowed with a soft, protective light.

"Who?" Max demanded.

Valeria shrugged. "I don't know. Wren and I can study the necklace while you find Rose."

Joshua hugged Serene and kissed her soundly. "Stay safe." He whispered something else Wren couldn't hear.

The magic from the necklace had been demonic in nature. What did demons have to do with Rose's issues?

15

———

VALERIA

Valeria stared at the tan walls of Master Phil's house. A possessed amulet had not been what she had expected when she volunteered to come with Wren. Although she was glad she had heeded her gut and followed. Somehow, all of this connected together.

She needed a plan. Her magic was very low. Probably too low to deal with any more black magic like what was in the amulet. Magic that reminded her strongly of the demonic powers she'd had when she had a demon soul bound to her own.

The similarities might not be a coincidence. For whatever reason, magic with ill intent tended to be black, red, or white when she saw the magic. She'd been more focused on freeing Joshua and getting the amulet in a protected space, but now her thoughts spiraled on what the connection could be. The only way to get some clues would be to investigate the amulet. As a witch with low power, she would need to make sure the preparation and mental space matched what she needed to do.

Serene hovered near Valeria. She cut a quick glance at Wren but straightened her shoulders. "Will Joshua be okay? Was he possessed?"

Valeria squeezed Serene's arm gently to reassure her. Alex had talked about Serene in an almost awed fashion. However they had met, she'd left a positive impression on Alex. Valeria's own observations had reinforced that this woman could be a friend. "Joshua was not possessed. Magic in the necklace compelled him to act a certain way. Made him want to protect you, I would guess."

"How do you know he wasn't possessed?"

Wren and Master Phil looked on with curiosity in their expressions but said nothing.

"Think of possession as levels. The first level is a spell like what we saw with Joshua. That is like a rock slide, trying to force him to do what the spell wanted. We all knew that something was wrong and, therefore, could fix it. That level also acts as a beacon for a demon spirit to come and take over. That would be the second level. The spirit could have laid hidden within Joshua and periodically come out to take action or influence him."

"Does he have a demon spirit in him now?" Serene's face lost its color, and she bit her lip.

Valeria squeezed Serene's arm again and released just a touch of power to make her feel calmer. "No, there was not enough time for one, and I also checked when the spell was broken. The demon would have been drawn to the surface with the broken spell."

Serene sighed and nodded. "So he is safe."

"From this, yes," Valeria said.

"What was the other level?" Master Phil asked, his expression alight with the curiosity of a lifelong student.

"The final level is when the demon within someone takes over completely. In that phase, the demon usually has access to all of the memories of the person they are controlling. They can act mostly like the other person until the time to strike arises."

"So more like an assassin?" Master Phil pulled the pot away from the fire so it could simmer. "If a demon had taken control, Joshua would have acted normal now and then later done something."

"Would the person remember the possession?" Serene asked.

"Probably not," Valeria said, remembering her own blank spots within her memories. Perhaps Max's memories were missing, in part, to demon possession.

"How do you get a demon out once it takes someone over?" Master Phil asked.

"It's not easy to do." Valeria dodged. While a demon always had a reason for the things that they did, there was always a master plan, according to what Isabella had taught Valeria. The stronger demons controlled the weaker ones. A demon would not just fully possess someone. The possession took too much energy, which was why her own family took the action of removing the human spirit from the body. That allowed the demon unfettered control of the body, and the demon would have access to its full powers.

"Thankfully, Joshua did not have that happen and is safe." Wren's kind and supportive words surprised Valeria.

"Thank you." Serene wiped away the tears. "This could have been so much worse without your help." She held Wren's and Valeria's gazes.

"We were glad to help. I'll make sure Joshua gets the bill." Wren grinned at Serene.

Serene jumped, but then a tentative smile formed on her lips. She must have realized he was joking. "Thanks, Wren."

"Serene and I will go to our contacts in the West Market. You are welcome to do your investigation here." Master Phil gestured around his home.

"Thank you. I know healers are different. Is there some payment that would offset the effort to clean afterward?" If she were using a witch's space, she would have some idea of what to do in thanks. A small trinket or some act to make the witch feel good would be appropriate. Her demon family had always wanted blood or pain. A healer was a different magical beast.

He gave a sad smile. "I have some herbs that a certain vendor will not readily sell to me."

"Tell me who and what and I shall get them," Valeria offered.

"I will." He and Serene left, closing the door and leaving Wren and Valeria alone in the house.

"You hesitated to answer her question about possession," Wren said after the door was closed.

"Demons are hard to remove once they fully possess someone. I didn't want her to know how close she probably came to losing Joshua."

Wren nodded. "What would we have done?"

"Once we knew for sure that he was possessed, the best way to remove a demon is to bring it to the spirit realm. Not many people can go there." She could go to that place as a witch, but very few other people could.

"The only way I know of to get to the spirit realm is if someone dies or is dying."

Valeria nodded. "The body does not last long without its soul."

"So you would have had to kill him in a way that was reversible, fight the demon in the spirit realm, and then bring the soul back to his body?"

"All within five minutes, maybe a few more minutes, before true death sets in." Valeria shuddered. She didn't mention that she didn't have the power to do anything like that now. The only time she had destroyed a demon that way was when the demon who had shared her body attacked her sister. Valeria had barely survived.

Wren shook himself. "What can I do to help? The magic acted as if it were coming from somewhere else." He closed his eyes. Perhaps that would give him a better recollection of what had happened. That tactic did help her.

"That describes what I saw. The magic wasn't fully in this world. I will need a spell circle." Where would such magic hide?

"Do witches always need a spell circle?" Wren's voice held no censure, just curiosity.

"Many spells are done without such preparation. If I need to be sure to focus my energy and intentions or I need a separate protected area to work, I would create a circle." Not to mention she needed to use less power.

Wren nodded and gestured toward the floor. "Mages are the same. How much space did you need?"

She pictured what spells she might cast to cleanse the necklace. None of them seemed as if they required much extra room. "Not too much in this case. The circle needs to be perhaps a foot wide."

He stepped toward the entryway. "This is where I would put the circle if I were casting the spell." The unasked question was loud between them.

The spot was perfect. She might even be able to get sunlight into the circle if she needed that power. There was enough room around where he had indicated for both of them to sit and hold hands. How did a mage select a spot? "Why here?"

His cheeks reddened and then he shrugged. "It felt right."

She grinned at him, liking his flush. "We could make a great witch out of you yet."

His shy smile back warmed her chest. She knelt on the floor to create the circle. Maybe there would be some residual spell she could see. She needed to center herself first before she started any magic. The puzzle of the necklace taunted her, making focus harder.

The fact that both she and Wren were brought into Rose and Max's magical woes was also very odd. Why would Alesia tell Serene to protect Rose? Why would Serene encourage Max to come to Wren when they had been fighting? Wren was a very powerful mage, but there were other magic users and other collections of mages who would have been just as powerful. Even how she and Wren first met by Meep invasion of the Archive was suspect. She was missing pieces.

And she could not get over the idea that the interactions linked together somehow, but the actual connection eluded her. The whole situation made her uneasy.

Wren watched her silently, seeming to be lost in his own thoughts.

"What did you sense?" Valeria asked.

Wren sighed. "Demonic magic."

Valeria shuddered at the confirmation of her own senses. Demon magic was too close to her own past. There had to be some other connection than generic demon magic. "How does Alesia's magic work?"

Wren blinked at her.

"She specifically told Serene to protect Rose, which brought the existence of this demonic magic to my attention. I get the sense that you and I were the only ones who might know about the demonic magic. But because the person who brought us together was Alesia, her involvement could imply a connection to our own problems."

"I don't know much about her magic. Alesia has helped our people as did my grandmother." He scowled, perhaps remembering what happened to his grandmother.

Was the fact Wren had never delved into Alesia's magic odd? "Have you ever looked at her when she was helping?"

Wren shook his head. "I was young when she first did her... magic and had not been trained enough to observe. Since then, she's not done her magic while I was around."

"But she seemed to use divination?" She needed some way to connect the events.

He shrugged. "She prevented things from going wrong. So possibly. You think she warned Serene so that she would come to us?"

"I think so. Which would imply Alesia wanted us to know that demonic magic is active with Rose and Max's issues." The words felt right. Her own intuition tingled.

"And you think demonic magic is possibly involved with my family's problems? That seems like a stretch."

"If Alesia couldn't come to you for some reason, but she needed you to see something, possibly without others knowing that she was giving hints..." She watched him to see if what she was implying was something Alesia might do.

"So something in the process of helping Rose and Max will reveal a clue to the prophecy."

Valeria shrugged. They were running out of time. There were many things they still didn't know. "Maybe. Or Alesia's involvement could be as simple as Rose or Serene being good friends with Alesia."

"Alesia is close to Serene. I'm not sure she knows Rose at all."

Valeria wasn't sure if Alesia's friendship with Serene helped explain why Alesia had brought them together. If there was a connection, the fact Alesia could not tell Wren directly must be significant. Alesia could have been far more subtle if she didn't want Valeria to know Alesia's involvement.

"Why would it matter if all of this is woven together?" Wren's voice broke her train of thought.

"The spell I am about to cast responds to my feelings and intentions. So not only am I trying to help find Rose and possibly help stop the evil mage who controls her, but I need insight into how this all relates to your issue." And possibly Valeria's own family issues. Not to mention she needed to do the spell with as little power as she could get away with.

Wren nodded. "Are you ready at this point?"

Valeria closed her eyes and blanked her mind and then focused on his question.

Yes. She was ready now. Taking a deep breath and releasing it made her feel slightly better. She opened her eyes and created a simple circle to protect them. The circle completed, she closed her eyes again and let the pull of the trance take over. The bells distinctly tinkled in the distance.

An image of the necklace she'd taken from Joshua appeared. Dark magic flowed, connecting back to something evil and malevolent. The vision cleared. Wren and she were on the right track thinking things were related.

She knelt and created an inner circle with enough room for them to sit between the lines. "Can you infuse some of your power to the circle?" Valeria asked as she sat cross-legged on one side of the circle. She took out the bagged necklace and slid the necklace out of the bag without touching it. The jewelry landed with a soft rattle in the center of the circle. She felt a hint of the same malevolent energy she had sensed earlier.

Wren sat next to her and gently gripped her hand. A subtle request to share power hit her magical senses.

She took what he offered and infused the circle with power.

Once the protective magic glowed around the inner circle, she reached her senses to the amulet.

Fragments of the spell still stuck on the necklace, but there was no overt power. The necklace had affected Joshua, so could there be a hidden spell? Or had the spell finally broken with removing the amulet from Joshua's grasp while mid-spell?

"I sense nothing," Wren said quietly.

"Do you think the spell could be triggered by the proximity to a person?"

"It's a good theory to test. Are you thinking of one of us touching the necklace?" Wren's lip curled. Mages were known for not getting their hands dirty. She tried not to let the slight affect her emotional state.

"There is something on your mind." She needed to get the negative energy removed if she was going to chance touching the amulet.

"Do you remember the truth circle with Max?"

Valeria was not sure what Wren was going to ask. "Yes?"

"Did my aura show anything odd?"

She thought back to the circle. She had been aware of his aura but had been completely focused on Max. The undead who had no idea he was undead. "No."

Wren scowled. "There is something wrong." The words came out strangled.

She reached for more of her power, and the small sounds of bells tingled in the background of her mind. She sent out a small bit of power to touch his hand.

"Is this about sleepwalking and the urge to see Alesia?"

"Yes." His mouth set to a firm, straight line. "Am I possessed like my sister?"

"The flame is not the same as any possession I have seen." She wondered what he was thinking. His face was so different from the normal expression he wore. The cockiness and pretense were gone. His eyes and mouth drooped with sadness, and his shoulders seemed to slump in defeat.

She knew he respected her, because of some of his actions, but she wasn't really sure what else he thought. In that moment, she realized this could be her chance to see the real Wren. "Tell me what happened."

He stared at the ground. "My sister was possessed because of me. It was my fault." His words were soft.

"How?"

"I let her go to the fortune teller. That's what started this. That is what consigned my sister to lose her mind from possession. Just like my grandmother." He stared down and then his back and shoulders stiffened. After a moment, he raised his gaze to meet hers.

The mixture of guilt, shame, and sadness took Valeria's breath away. "You blame yourself for things that are not your fault."

His lips pressed together. He didn't believe her.

"I come from a family who was possessed. Nothing I did started that. My grandmother, Isabella, was evil and did evil things. Does that make me evil?" Her answer of "no" had been a hard-won battle.

Wren stared at her.

Valeria squeezed his hand. "We have to find the root of what happened." They needed to clear the air so they could figure out what was going on with the amulet.

"What do you need to know?" Wren asked gruffly.

"Was your grandmother the first?" she asked.

"Maybe." Wren seemed to study her face. "How did you find out your family was possessed?"

She'd never told anyone about her family. His expression told her he would be offended if she didn't tell him. The idea that she might be able to hurt his feelings was so strange. He'd seemed so impervious to everything, and they had only just met.

Valeria sighed. "I found out after I thought my sister had died. She really had escaped from the demons. My grandmother had separated us after an episode...." She thought about the events of her life. Wren and she shared some similarities. For years, she had blamed herself for her sister's fate. "I blamed myself for the separation. Because I didn't stop her from doing something she wanted to do." Corona had coaxed Valeria out of bed to see the dawn magic and observe how their eyes changed colors. Isabella had caught and punished them both.

Valeria tilted her head and smiled at him, hoping he could see the similarity in their stories.

He nodded. "But your separation from Corona was not what was to blame for your family's situation?"

"No, my family had been cursed years before. I found out later that the fate of my family was changed by Isabella." Valeria couldn't help wondering what the effect of Wren's guilt was on his life and even his magic.

"Before we start the spell, I meant to give this to you sooner." Wren removed two charms from his bag. "These will help your sister and niece."

"Thank you." Her fingers brushed his, and warmth settled in her chest.

He gave her a quick but real grin. "How did you find out about your family?"

"My sister and her husband. They have an extensive library. She married into a family of scholars. Do we know what possessed Alesia?" Most possessions were demonic in nature.

"No. The being possessing Alesia has helped us in the past. The city would have burned and been invaded by the neighboring town." Wren shook his head and then shrugged. He must know how odd that was.

Valeria had no real knowledge of the history around her. She'd been so isolated growing up. Even now, she was more focused on the here and now. But saving a town from invasion did not sound like what a demon would do. The likelihood that Alesia was not possessed by a demon made Valeria feel better.

Without overthinking it too much, Valeria reached out and touched the amulet. At first, nothing happened. Then a tattoo on her arm that was protection specific to demons flashed, and she heard the faint tinkling of bells coming closer and closer until they stopped. The smell of cinnamon and freshly baked bread replaced the faint antiseptic and wet-dog smell in the room.

The amulet crackled and turned to dust. Their lead to what was going on was lost.

16

WREN

Wren stared at the pile of dust in the middle of the spell circle.

"That was not what I was hoping for." Valeria shut and rubbed her eyes. Her fingers shook. The fragments of the necklace disappeared into Master Phil's floor, leaving no trace the necklace had even existed.

"What happened?" Wren kept his voice soft.

She sighed. "I'm not sure. Maybe I was too tired to be casting such a delicate spell. My protective magic flared because the necklace was about to attack me."

"We are not going to be any good to anyone if we don't get some rest." Wren tried to work through options. There were not many.

"Do you think they will find Rose today?" Valeria stood and then sat in a chair by the hearth. Her eyes fluttered shut. Even exhausted, she was one of the most intriguing females he had ever encountered.

"If they do, I'm not sure how much help I can be." Wren sat in a chair opposite her. The steady warmth of the fire and the faint smell of stew relaxed him further. He could sleep right here in a stranger's house.

"Yeah, me either."

"What if we take a short nap? And..." Wren pursed his lips. A short nap was not going to help him much. He needed solid, high quality sleep to regain his powers. With how tired he was, he would be even more prone to sleepwalk. Valeria in her current state might not be able to watch him. Neither one of them had enough energy to set anything but the most rudimentary wards. That would leave them both vulnerable. More vulnerable than he had been since he was a kid.

"Alex mentioned that there was an emergency way to recharge energies."

Wren cocked his head and thought back through the conversations he had had with Alex. In their years of friendship, Wren didn't remember anything like that. "How did that come up?"

"We were talking about defensive magic. Corona has many in-laws, but they are only minor mages. If their place is attacked, her in-laws will have to awaken everyone. That will disrupt their sleep. If the attacks keep coming, the defenders may no longer have enough power to keep fighting. After each attack is vanquished, they are even more vulnerable to attack. He had something in the Archive that could help with that."

Wren nodded and then yawned.

Valeria yawned back and then laughed. "Why don't we see if he has anything that we could use? If I sit here any longer, I am going to fall asleep. I don't think that is wise." She wiggled her eyebrows. "Are you going to fly us?"

Even though his body felt heavy, Wren laughed. "Yes. It would be better than walking."

He made sure to close the door behind him. He swept Valeria off her feet and launched himself into the air. The trip to the Archive was done in silence. He glanced down. Valeria snoozed in his arms.

At least with flying, he was not going to fall asleep. The city blurred with a blink.

He landed in the Archive's courtyard. When he set her down, Valeria gave him a sleepy smile and led the way through the main door. The archive's guardian demon was still not at the desk. He glanced at Valeria and wondered if she would truly respond that badly to a demon. "Are you able to sense demons?"

"Yes, as long as my senses are not blinded, I can tell when a demon gets close." Valeria tapped a place on her forearm. He knew she had hidden tattoos. She must be tapping the one that sensed demons.

"Have you ever met a good demon?"

"No." The finality in her words made him understand why the Archive's guardian might make herself scarce. At some point he was going to need to introduce them, since they were on the same side.

"Where do you think Alex is?"

"By the egg." Valeria hurried to the back where they had cast the spell on the Meeps.

Alex lay in a bedroll surrounded by a stack of books and near the dragon egg. The egg looked exactly the same.

"Wren? Valeria? What are you doing here?" Alex jumped up from his bedroll and flushed. The small whirl of dust swirling by his feet indicated his nervousness.

"You mentioned once that the Archive might have a way to recharge magical energy." Valeria stepped closer and laid her hand on the egg. After a moment, she smiled. "The egg is doing fine."

Alex's shoulders relaxed. "I would feel better if the egg..." He froze, seeming lost in his thoughts. After a few minutes, he shook himself. "The defensive recharge we talked about is only for a many defender situation, but I think...Follow me."

Valeria stepped close to Wren. Her breath was warm on his chin. "Any idea what he is talking about?"

Wren shook his head. Alex had so much knowledge in his head that sometimes the information came together in odd ways. "Nope, but I think whatever he thought of will help us."

"Come on! There's a room you have not been to." Alex hurried away and after some twists and turns, Alex led them to a tunnel Wren had never been down before. The air was thick with dust and disuse as if they were the first people to go down the hall in a long, long time.

The corridor opened into a small circular, stone room. The room had the rounded edges of a nesting room in the Rookery. On a shelf on the far side was an alcove with a chest.

Alex stepped inside.

Wren crashed against an invisible barrier, stubbing his toe and hitting his shoulder. "Ouch."

"What's wrong?" Valeria touched his arm.

"I'm blocked from entering." Wren ran his hands along the solid, invisible wall. His magical senses also saw nothing.

"Oh, I didn't expect that since the Archive said this room was set up by Kamali," Alex murmured, looking back at Wren.

Wren's heart stopped, and he grabbed Alex's arm. "My grandmother had this room created?"

Alex nodded. "If Kamali is your grandmother, then yes. The records noted that she came every day for two months to complete the room."

Wren searched his mind but had not seen a record of his

grandmother contributing to the Archive. She was not known as a scholar. There were some general notes that his people had helped establish the Archive just after the Merge. "Did she leave a message?"

Alex shook his head. "Not that I have seen."

"If this is related to the prophecy, then maybe I need to try." Valeria stepped past him, hands raised as if expecting to hit a wall, but she passed through the barrier. "You need to be a witch to pass. Let's combine our magic."

Wren hesitated. Why could Alex get through, when he was not a witch? Perhaps his position as an archivist allowed him to enter. Wren took a step away from the invisible wall.

She crossed back over the barrier and then turned and faced him. Her back toward the barrier, she took his hands, gazing into his eyes. Magic shivered up his spine, and his magic connected to Valeria's with no issue. Her eyes widened and her lips parted. He could almost feel her surprise.

Valeria backed up a step and then two until they were both in the center of the room. The air shimmered around them. The overwhelming feeling of being safe and protected blanketed him. His shoulders relaxed, and he felt as if he had given his burdens to a trusted friend. By the tense set of Alex's shoulders, he must be the only one affected.

"What is this place?" Wren turned in place. The plain, bare walls were stone. Visually, there didn't seem to be anything remarkable here.

Alex shrugged. "I don't know anything other than that Kamali created the chamber. I also realized that this would make an ideal location for the dragon egg."

Valeria nodded. "The room is solid, stone, and protected. That would make this place perfect for the egg. It almost feels like a sacred place, but there is something odd. Alex, what did she do in here?"

"The record only said she embedded magic in the walls that was reusable."

"Reusable?" Valeria reached out and touched the wall. "The magic is just below the surface."

The strange feeling in the air grew as he looked around. Anticipation? "I don't know anything about mining magic and replenishing my personal stores." Sharing power between magical people, sure, but the amount of power between the two mages went down. The cost of the exchange used some power. So the result was less magic between the two mages.

Valeria pursed her lips. "Do you think adding power would work the way I added back your soul?"

Wren jerked his arm away from the wall. His heart pounded. He examined Valeria, whose face went red. "Considering you never actually told me about that, I have no idea."

"His soul?" Alex snapped to attention, his eyes wide.

"You tell him. I want to hear how the spell affected you." Valeria crossed her arms, and she raised her brows in challenge.

Wren told Alex about discovering his fire, the spell his grandmother had left, the way the spell had hurt, and even that Blackie had disrupted the spell.

"Who is Blackie?" Alex asked.

"A nuisance of a dog that came with a student who lives in the Rookery," Wren groused. The dog had not gotten into the eggs, but he had shown up in so many unexpected places with an apologetic Rye trailing after him.

"When Wren was unconscious after the spell, Rye and I reattached the flame and the soul pieces he had lost." She glanced at him, probably wondering if he was going to be angry.

Was that why he had felt physically good after the spell?

Alex huffed and pushed Wren's shoulder. "You could have died."

Wren flushed, but he would die for his family and that was the same then as it was now. "Dying isn't my first choice."

Alex crossed his arms and frowned at Wren. Now they both looked angry. The wind picked up around them, letting Wren know how upset Alex really was.

"I'm not going to feel bad about this. I want us to solve the prophecy. And to live long enough to get a book in the Archives." When neither one's expression changed, Wren decided to point out their own hypocrisy. "Tell me you each don't have people you would die for."

Valeria sagged and then nodded. "Alex, tell us about the room?"

Alex shot Wren a dirty look and then focused his attention on Valeria. "The record said there was magic layered in the walls that could be used to replenish a magical supply."

Wren put his hand on the wall and closed his eyes. Very faintly, he could feel the flow of power.

"It feels the way your fire does. Like it's sleeping," Valeria said.

"So what do we do to wake it up?" Alex asked.

"I'm not sure, but I know a spell for creating a passage for magic. It's like a tunnel. The spell was designed to drain excess spell's energy from an apprentice's mistake." Wren had that particular spell used on him often as a teen.

Valeria put her hand back on the wall. "That might work. So you have experience?"

"We used that spell on the cursed sword." Wren said. The spell hadn't been that hard. Tunneling and moving magic required a bunch of power..

Alex laughed. "That was the spell? Yeah, that spell broke the curse and funneled off the power."

"Wait. Tell me that wasn't the sword you gave me." Valeria's eyes narrowed and her lips pursed. "The one you said to use to defend against the Meeps?"

Alex covered his face. "I panicked. It seemed like a good idea."

The image of Alex handing a sword to Valeria struck Wren as funny. Especially since the sword was a formerly cursed one. "He gave *y-you* a sword?" Wren laughed.

Valeria's giggle was sweet and made Wren want to hug her.

"I just stuck the sword back on the shelf. I'm glad I didn't try anything. With my luck, I might have reactivated the curse." Valeria giggled again, covering her face with her hand.

Alex huffed. "Anyway. You should be able to pull out the power from the walls to create the tunnel and funnel the magic back into your personal stores. You would have to do the incantation with Valeria."

"Why?" Wren was not opposed to working with Valeria.

"Because the room is keyed to witch's magic," Alex said.

Wren blinked. The idea that only witches could enter was odd enough. Why would his grandmother do such a thing? He'd never heard of witches working with the Aeros. Had his grandmother somehow divined that they would need the energy and that he would be with a witch?

"The best way I know of moving power is through dance." Valeria watched Wren, probably waiting to see his freak-out about dancing.

Wren shrugged. He hated dancing, but sometimes the spells called for movement, and dance was a good way to make that happen. "It would probably be easier to do the tunneling as a part of the dance."

She grinned. Her smile was so full of mischief and delight he knew he must be smiling back.

"Maybe we are meant to use this spell on your sister," Valeria said softly as if she could sense how much he didn't want to make a fool of himself in front of her.

He couldn't imagine needing such a spell for his sister, but he nodded. If he had been willing to die, he had to be willing to dance. Although which would be worse was a close call.

He let out his breath and stepped to the middle of the room.

"How does this work?" Valeria handed her bag to Alex and stood facing Wren.

"The spell is simple. You have to bounce magic and leave trails that form a web. Once you have the web, we are going to move the magic to the web. Then we will do what you suggested and dance to transfer power." If they messed up, the wards and solid stone should keep the Archive safe. He waved Alex out. The spell was probably safer if just Wren and Valeria were in the room.

Valeria made a face at the word web, but she nodded.

"Come hold my hands. It would be easier to show you. This doesn't take a lot of power, but it does take focus and cooperation."

She stood in front of him and held out her hands. The level of trust shocked him. They had not met that long ago and not under the best of circumstances. Here she was not even a day later and willing to merge their magic in a major unknown spell. The trust took his breath away and brought warmth to his chest.

Wren shook off the extra emotions and took her hands in his, interlacing their fingers. He connected his magic easily as if they had been exchanging magic for years. He decided to worry about why connecting with Valeria was so easy later. The power swirled in a mix of gold and blue. Even pooling their power, there was not much left.

He carefully took a small mix of both of their energies and then pictured the magic as a ball. When the magic obeyed and formed a small orb, he tossed the magic to bounce off of the chamber's walls. A thin steak of magic formed a trail behind the sphere, leaving a faint glow. He created another ball and threw that one too.

"Should I start?"

"Anytime that feels right."

Valeria smirked and her eyes sparkled. She created her own orbs that he tossed against the walls. Soon the room was filled with hundreds of tiny spheres that ricocheted around the room. The thin strands of power stretched across the space, surrounding them.

Once the room hummed with the bouncing balls, he released her hand. "Now we have to dance."

He focused his breathing and thoughts on replenishing his power to help save and protect Rose, Max, Alesia, Alex, Valeria. There were more he wished to protect, but when thinking Valeria's name, he could feel the way the magic wanted him to move. This was not a mage-like reaction but a witch's. His carefully locked-away emotions spilled into the magic. He let them, understanding this was the only way the spell would work. Not only would he die or dance to save his sister, he would allow his emotions to be his guide and cast spells like a witch.

His body took over, and he lost himself in the magic, feeling better and better with each step.

The magic in the room dissipated, leaving him humming with power. He felt as if he had gotten a full night's sleep. Valeria's eyes sparkled. Her face was open and vibrant. Her aura burst with power.

Reluctantly, he released his connection with Valeria. A shiver of cold raised the feathers on his neck. He'd never felt cold before when breaking the connection with another. He'd always been relieved. That must be a witch thing.

"Did it work?" Alex called from the door.

Wren nodded. "I feel great."

"Can we see what's in the box now?" Alex stepped into the room.

In Wren's focus, he'd completely forgotten about the chest. Maybe the chest had more of his grandmother's writing. There could be clues to what the prophecy meant. He reached to open the chest, but the alcove, shelf, and chest disappeared as he touched it.

"What in the world?" Alex was by Wren's side and ran his hands over the walls. The tingle of earth magic sparked in the air.

"What do you sense?" Wren pressed the palm of his hand to the wall. The stone seemed solid, and it was as if the chest had never existed.

"This is ancient rock." Alex's brows furrowed in concentration.

"What else do you sense?" Valeria stood on the other side of Alex.

"This is untouched rock. Powerful and solid."

"Meaning the chest was an illusion?" Valeria asked.

Alex nodded and walked a circuit around the room. "Everything around me is ancient rock."

Why would his grandmother leave such a trick? He glanced at Alex, who was still doing a slow circuit of the room. Without the chest, would Alex be examining the room so closely? The fake chest might not even have been for Wren.

He shivered and glanced at Valeria. Her lip caught in her teeth. She seemed deep in thought. The last time he had felt the urge to give into his silly desires, he'd uncovered another clue. This urge probably would not help him now but might help Alex.

"This room is shaped like a nesting room." Wren pointed to the rounded edges and the concave floor.

"You don't think the egg would suffer because of the magic

still in the walls?" Alex asked over his shoulder.

"I feel no trace of anything but protective magic. An ideal place for the egg." Valeria met Wren's gaze with a strange expression on her face.

Alex glanced around the room again and nodded. His inward gaze said the nod was not for Wren or Valeria.

"Did my grandmother leave anything else?" Wren watched Alex carefully.

Alex shook himself. "No, just this room."

Wren wasn't surprised. The fact that he had topped-off magical power and felt as if he had slept for a full day was an incredible outcome of their visit. He'd still hoped for a message from his grandmother to say he was doing what he should. With only a day left before their thirtieth birthdays, hopefully this side trip would somehow help his sister. "What now?"

"This room gave me an idea on how we might deal with Rose when we find her." Valeria said. "We need a circle that would create the web and allow us to funnel the magic more quickly."

Wren remembered the kick Rose hit Max with. "We also need to be outside the circle in case she fights us."

Valeria nodded her head slowly. "I think the idea will work. I just need to know where Rose will be with enough time to set up the circle. She will need to be in the circle to break the control and disperse the spell's power."

"Let's find the others." Wren turned to thank Alex, but he was gone. Hopefully, whatever Wren had set in motion would help Alex.

Wren resisted the urge to take Valeria's hand as they walked out of the Archive. The quiet halls gave him a moment to think.

His grandmother's actions worried him on some level. Was he but a puppet to her machinations? That thought didn't feel right. He had not been compelled to support that the room was a good place for the egg. His grandmother had seemed to set up the circumstances so that he would naturally agree. The room was good. He could have chosen to not comment or even point out the apparent manipulation by his grandmother. Not really his grandmother, but the entity who possessed her and could see the future.

"Someone with a glimpse into the future must have known the tools we'd need," Valeria said as they stepped out of the Archive. Her thoughts being such a mirror of his own made him groan. Had he said his idea out loud?

"Does it bother you?" Wren waved his hands to encompass everything.

Instead of laughing or poking fun, Valeria laid her hand on his arm. "There are many people trying to influence me and my actions. All I can do is try to make the best choices with what I know. I can keep trying to do good."

Something in Wren's chest loosened.

"There you are." Serene grabbed Valeria's arm. "We found her. You have to hurry."

17

VALERIA

Evening, Primum second, 300 years post-Merge

A few hours later...

Valeria hid in the bushes. If everything went to plan, Master Phil would draw Rose away from her captors. She was being forced to lead a zombie army against the city. Why the mages thought that was a good idea, Valeria had no idea.

All she cared about was getting Rose in the modified spell circle. With Wren's help, she'd created a dome that used the ambient magic from inside to create the sticky web. The web itself would pull more power. When the web was thick enough, the magic would be strong enough to break most bonds. Then Valeria and Wren would use a modified form of the tunnel spell to disperse the magic from outside the ring. They still had to dance to cast that part of the spell.

Worry twisted her gut. There had not been much time to practice, and so many things could go wrong. If there was too much magic, the circle could explode. Depending on the level of power, an exploding circle could do anything from hurt those nearby to destroy most of the nearby city.

Wren's fire troubled her as well. She hadn't told Wren that many of the protective measures in his grandmother's room in the Archive were against fire. Whether those spells were for Wren or a potential dragon hatchling were not clear. Wren's fire had been unpredictable and could interfere with this ring. He would be on the outside and potentially put the people and forest at risk.

A splash distracted her. Rose must be close. Valeria had no time for changes or for second guessing.

The branches parted, and Rose stepped into the clearing. No zombies followed her. Valeria could see a glimpse of her pale face under her wild hair. The set of her shoulders made her look determined, but she froze at the edge of the clearing facing the spell circle.

Come on. I need you in the circle to help.

The moments ticked by. Valeria held her breath. If Rose didn't enter the ring, there was nothing Valeria could do.

Master Phil stepped from the wood and held out his hand to Rose. "You must come over here." His tone was soft and beguiling. He stood in front of the ring.

Rose's body loosened. She took a half step toward Master Phil. Rose's gaze shifted, and she blurred into motion. Before Valeria could even think about shouting a warning, Rose had tackled Master Phil and propelled them both into the spell circle.

The flash of magic through her link to the spell brought Valeria to her knees. Her ears rang, and the world blurred. She had expected far less magic. The spell would weave the power into an internal web. Hopefully that would hold the extra power.

Wren held her shoulder, and a soothing balm covered her skin. The ringing subsided. She blinked.

Rose and a strange man circled each other in the clearing. The wildness of his hair and spittle dripping from his mouth made Valeria think she'd missed most of the battle. His burnt, tattered robes flared around him, exposing a glowing necklace. Even without her magic sight engaged, the power of that necklace stunned her. His left hand gripped a sword dripping with blood. This must be the powerful mage involved with Rose and Max's troubles.

How long had Valeria been dazed?

"What—" Valeria shook her head, trying to focus.

"Goddess. Rose is going to knock the mage into the spell circle." Wren pulled Valeria to her feet. The world spun.

Valeria turned in time to see lightning whiz from the man's fingers. His face twisted in a scowl when it missed Rose.

The circle had barely survived Rose's magic. The internal web was now thick with energy. The spell would not hold up against what looked to be a formidable mage and his powerful necklace. Another magical onslaught would cause the worst case. The collapse of her circle would destroy most of the woods and part of the town.

Something about the situation made Valeria feel that the pool of such immense power was done for a reason. That much power could be used to...*and break open fully the portal to the Abyss.* The words of the prophecy echoed in her head.

Her heart slammed to life. She took a deep breath. Her focus needed to be on doing what she could to protect the world, her town, her friends, and Wren from the magical onslaught. The only thing she could control was her reaction.

Valeria stepped through the bushes just in time to see Rose rush forward and tackle the man into the circle.

The magical sonic boom shook Valeria. The spell strained against the black energy just under the surface of the other magical powers.

Valeria took a single step into the clearing when a female shriek startled Valeria.

A female dressed in dirty robes screamed and jumped into the ring. The added power sent a shock wave through the clearing. There was too much power from what had to be a second mage.

Fear and shock squeezed Valeria's chest. Only years of training kept her moving forward. There were only moments to do what she needed to do before the bond broke and more power overloaded the magic.

She ran to the edge of the circle, facing a pale-faced Wren.

"Wren, remember what we practiced for your sister?" Valeria hoped he would follow her lead and use the emotions he had for his sister to once again channel power.

Wren nodded calmly. Valeria reached out with her power and connected to Wren's magical center. Then she immersed herself in the wild rhythms of life.

Valeria weaved her arms in a sinuous and complicated pattern as her body swayed to some internal beat. Wren shot out his wings and executed flips and rolls that had him touching the branches of the trees. The words flowed through her. She knew that he said the same words.

Both their magical stores were full. She channeled as much power as she dared into the necklaces she sensed in the circle. The air crackled with too much power. Alex and the dragon egg popped into her mind. Hoping she was doing the right thing, she funneled magic toward both of them through the bonds of friendship Wren and she had with Alex.

She needed an outlet for the last of the released energy. Physical movement burned the most power. She sent a warning down her connection to Wren and let the power of the spell toss her and Wren into the woods.

She stole extra magic to cushion her fall. The pile of leaves crackled as she landed.

She spit out a crunchy leaf. The woods were quiet around her. If she had failed, there would be much more noise. Right? Doubt had her struggling to her feet. Maybe she was deaf and could not hear the bedlam.

Wren was at her side, helping her stand up. "Let's go help the others."

He pulled her back toward the clearing and through the bushes. Valeria stumbled. Noodles would have an easier time keeping her upright. Wren caught her before she could fall. She leaned against him. She didn't look too closely at the crispy remains in the circle.

"You guys okay?" Max asked.

Valeria jerked and turned to face him. Her senses were off, and she hadn't noticed anyone else in the clearing. Her face heated, and she leaned closer to Wren. There was no sign of Joshua or Serene. Max must have been close by, because he cradled Rose in his arms. She was tucked up on his lap. He dropped an empty potion bottle. He must have just given the potion to Rose. Next to them, Master Phil rummaged in his bag.

"This is normal after a big spell." Wren's voice croaked.

Valeria nodded and winced as the pain sliced through her head and neck. She moved her neck slowly.

"Is everyone okay?" Wren glanced around the group.

Master Phil muttered, "Yes" without looking away from his bag.

"It's a good thing I pulled my wings in. That would have broken them." Wren brushed some twigs off his feathers and rolled his shoulders. He seemed to be trying to put the group at ease.

"You just needed to land in a nice, soft pile of leaves." Valeria patted her hair, playing along. She sighed at the leaves she found in her hair.

Wren scowled at her before grinning. "After all that, did you use magic to break your fall? That's amazing."

Valeria grinned at him and then turned to look at the spell circle. "We set the spell to break any bonds on a person who entered the ring. There's always energy when breaking bonds. We hadn't expected that much energy. They must have had a bond to the shield as well as to each other." Her words were mostly true, if an oversimplification of what actually happened. If anyone were a scholar or had an interest in magic, she might have explained the differences in the order of what actually happened.

"We felt the shield come down, but there was no extra energy in the world at large," Wren said. Valeria glanced at Wren. Had he felt the shield go down? She hadn't. The shield around Hope being down would explain the extra power in the necklaces.

"They must have put the energy into the necklaces." Max pointed at the glowing stones.

Valeria picked her way over and used her blessed handkerchief to pull the necklaces off of what was left of the two skeletal mages.

"What will you do with them?" Wren asked.

Valeria knew he meant the necklaces. "Maybe they should go to the Archive." She tucked them into her bag. Perhaps once she determined that these necklaces would not be needed, they would end up in the Archive. So that was not quite a lie.

Rose stirred in Max's arms. "You're still alive."

"Still kicking." Max helped her sit up.

"What happened?" Rose looked dazed.

"The spell broke their control over you," Max said.

Valeria sat beside Rose. "Yes, we used what we learned about Max to construct a spell circle which would remove their control. We had to make some changes, so we weren't in the ring. Seemed like a wise move, since you may have tried to kill us." Valeria winked at Rose.

Rose's smile faltered. "The bond was so tight. I did what I could to help you save the town. I had to stab Max and lead the army. But I stabbed Max in a place he would recover from. And I didn't tell Calder the plan that would have taken the city." If Valeria had not been sitting so close, she would not have heard Rose's words.

Valeria had not been present for most of the action. Calder must be the name of the first mage to land in the circle and Rose must have stabbed Max earlier. He was undead, so unless she stabbed him in the heart, he would be able to recover fairly quickly.

Wren smiled and helped Valeria stand up. "You did good. I know you could have won. Joshua says you were the only one who could beat him at chess."

Master Phil still hunched over his bag. The stiff set of Master Phil's shoulders as he fiddled with his bag distracted Valeria. The sadness and resignation was apparent in the way he sat. He didn't seem to realize that Max and Rose were like siblings. She recognized that bond well. Or maybe there was something more at play. Master Phil was a wolf.

Valeria touched Master Phil's arm. "Are you okay? The spell would have broken any sort of bond. Even pack bonds."

Master Phil smiled sadly. "I have no bonds to break. I should go see if there are any wounded people in town." He left the clearing quickly without glancing back. Valeria's gaze followed him. If only she could help him. Wren stepped into her view and nodded toward the bushes.

The rest of the people seemed caught up in conversation, so she followed Wren away from the rest of their party.

"Did you see what I saw?" Wren watched her face.

Valeria thought back through everything that had happened. What would put that look on his face? "What did you see?"

"A thread of demonic power embedded in all of the amulets." Wren searched her gaze. "What will you really do with the pendants?"

Any demonic powers would have been cleared in anything within the ring. Valeria closed the pouch the pendants were in. "It feels like we will need them soon."

"What would we use them for?"

"Think of them as a magical energy source," Valeria said.

Wren raised his brows, asking silently for more information.

She sighed. "I'm not sure, but my intuition says we may need them."

Wren nodded, his brow furrowed in thought. "I think we should go back to the Rookery and make sure everyone is okay."

"Do you think the undead made it to the city?" Valeria asked. Wren seemed genuinely worried.

"No, but the demons involved with this could have used the attack as a diversion."

Valeria still didn't understand how everything fit together. "Maybe. But I think that the demons have a few other plans to open the Abyss." There had been too much power in the circle. That level of power might only be seen once a millennium.

"How are the demons involved with my family's curse?" Wren's voice snapped and his whole body language, from the feathers on his head to the tension in his shoulders screamed anger and confusion.

She put her hand on his arm. His shoulders relaxed.

"Let's go back to the Rookery."

He nodded but would not quite meet her gaze. Valeria would reach out later to the group. Her intuition said she needed to be at the Rookery. The walk back didn't bring her any insights as to why. Once inside, Wren flapped up and away.

She walked up the stairs, stopping to stretch every floor. Maybe she could create a permanent magical way that anyone could use to get up the Rookery? She had no idea if that would be allowed.

At the fiftieth floor, Rye bounded down the stairs. The black dog was nowhere in sight. "I'm so glad I found you." Rye seemed a little bit worried.

Valeria sat and patted the stair next to her. "What's wrong?"

Rye held out a red slip of paper. "This is from the Archive."

The note read:

The babe comes early. W.

W for William, Corona's husband. Fear choked Valeria. She hadn't gotten the protective charms to her sister yet. If the baby came before Valeria could get there, the demons would be able to find her niece. Valeria's pack still held the charms Wren had given her after their disastrous fire removal spell. "Tell Wren."

Before Rye could say anything, Valeria raced down the stairs.

If only she would have brought the amulet to her sister as soon as Valeria had gotten them. She thought she had time.

Corona's house was hidden from the air. Between that and the darkness, running would be faster. She hit the cobbled street and used one of her tattoos to increase her speed.

Valeria prayed she was not too late.

18

———

WREN

Evening, Primum second, 300 years post-Merge

Wren focused on the letter's words. The stack of correspondence on his desk was a foot tall. He sighed and rubbed his eyes. The Rookery was fine. Everything was fine, but the sense that something was wrong continued to grow. Nothing made sense.

"Wren!" Rye busted in the door and ran to his desk. She wrung her hands and fidgeted.

"What's wrong?" He stood up.

A flashed of what looked like guilt crossed her face.

The issue must be about her dog. "Is it Blackie?"

She nodded, and a glint of tears shone in her eyes. "He won't leave the room."

Wren sighed and debated sending his assistant to help her. "What room?"

"The one the fire removal spell was done in."

Wren stiffened. "How did you get the door open?"

"It was unlocked." Rye shrugged, but the redness in her face said that was a lie.

What in the world was going on? "Let's go."

As they walked down the stairs, Rye started to cry. "I didn't mean to cause so much trouble. Blackie saved my life. I had to help him..." Her words grew less coherent as she walked.

Wren strode through the short hall to the open door into the phoenix room. Lying in the middle of the spell circle was Alesia. Her blonde hair cascaded across the floor. Her face was pale and her eyes were shut. Her hands and white wings were bound by dark cords.

A sack like one a person might get a delivery from was crumpled up in the corner. A feather sat by the sack's opening. Someone must have gotten to Alesia, kidnapped her, and then brought her here. But how? She was well protected in Walter's burrows, and she had her own type of protection with the seer who possessed her.

The urge to touch Alesia pulled him across the room. Where was the dog? Something was wrong.

Malevolence cloaked in innocence draws us together. Its victory will be our failure.

He hesitated, closing his fist. Why was the draw to touch her so strong? The urge was even more powerful than normal. Unnaturally strong.

Two halves united shall burn and be reborn

Were he and Alesia the two halves? If so, what was trying to force them together?

and break open fully the portal to the Abyss.

The last line implied that the force could be demonic in nature. Wren took a step back. He needed to find Valeria.

"Lock the door." A deep voice growled from the darkest corner of the room.

Rye shut and locked the door. She collapsed against it. "You promised to let him go."

"Foolish girl. Why would I let go of such a useful body?" Blackie stepped out of the shadows.

The air snapped with rage and malevolence. The dog doubled in size, and the black hair merged into long spikes off of his back. The skin lightened and morphed into pebbled white scales. The dog's eyes flamed.

The fire within Wren's body rose to the surface, tingling across his skin. He stepped over to put himself between the demon and Alesia.

"Wren, don't touch your sister. That's what they want you to do!" Rye shouted.

Her words reminded him of when Rye and he had been alone in the room. She had tried to tell him about Blackie. She'd stopped when the dog had entered the room. Rye was an unwilling participant, which meant he needed to protect her.

The urge to touch Alesia was like a living thing twisting in his chest. Not only did he want to check to make sure she was okay, but he felt almost driven to give her a hug.

The demon took a menacing step forward. Wren took one back. He still didn't understand what was going on. Why did the demon want him to touch his sister? Why was there a compulsion to do so? Why was the fire in his bones building? At some point, even in this room, his fire could become a danger to the rest of the Rookery.

An idea took shape. If he could get Rye and Alesia safe, he could use his flames to kill the demon.

The spell circle was to the side of the floor and was still set-up to resist flames from when Valeria tried to remove the fire within him. His plan required getting Rye in the protected ring with Alesia.

He slid away from the demon-dog so that there would be

room for Rye to get to the circle. "Rye, I need you to check on Alesia." He used his no-nonsense voice with her.

She glanced at the demon-dog and nodded. She swayed as she stood and crept along the wall toward Alesia. Once she was inside the protected area, he sent the faintest stream of power to activate the magic.

Once he felt the shield engage, he let loose the control he had on the flames within him. His skin heated. Flames surrounded Wren. The fire ran up and down his skin without burning him. He knew instinctively that he was not immune to the flames, but he just had a high tolerance for heat. He was going to test that now.

The demon laughed. "Do you think a little flame will hurt me?"

"No, but a lot might." Wren focused on increasing his flame. Fire surged around him, getting hotter and hotter. He felt no pain, only resignation. With his sister safely in the ring, even if he died killing the monster, she would be saved.

The fire kicked up, and the demon scrambled away. Wren caught the creature by his back leg and held on. The fiend howled as the flames crept up its body. The fiend twisted and bucked, throwing Wren. He landed hard, his breath whooshing out.

The demon crawled toward the spell circle. He could be powerful enough to break the protection and kill Alesia and Rye. There was no way Wren would let him.

Wren gritted his teeth against the pain of sitting up and leapt forward, tackling the monster. He landed on top of the fiend. Wren focused his flames on the demon below him. The demon's body shifted to ash beneath Wren. He tried to pull the flames back, but he couldn't. The first lick of pain hit his system. His flames were more than whatever protection he had.

Sweat poured down his face. He could still breathe, but his

lungs burned with each inhale. He fought the flames for control. Too much flame and his sister would die. His heart raced, which only seemed to inspire the flames to rise higher.

"Alesia, no!" Rye shrieked. "Woof!"

A flare of magic below him meant the Woof must have been a spell activation word.

A small, cool hand landed on his shoulder. His fire jerked and flowed toward something behind him.

"It is time," Alesia said.

The world went up in flames.

19

VALERIA

<u>Night, Primum second, 300 years post-Merge</u>

Valeria slammed open the front door of the home Corona had been hiding in. "Corona!"

Corona came to the door with her dark hair in disarray and her round cheeks flushed. She stopped when she saw Valeria. "What's wrong?"

Valeria reached to rest her hand on her sister's much bigger baby belly. The surface rippled with the baby's movement. She let out a little magic to feel the baby. Her niece was fine and not quite ready to come out of the womb. The relief of that fact coursed through Valeria and weakened her legs. She was not too late.

"The baby is fine." Corona rubbed her hand up and down Valeria's back.

"Take this. It's the charm that Wren gave me to hide you and the baby from demons." Valeria dug into her bag and pulled out the charms. Just in case anything happened to her, she needed Corona and her niece safe.

Corona slipped the charm on and tucked the other in her pocket. Her face pinched with worry. "Thank you. But why are you here?"

"I had a note from the Archive that the baby was coming too soon."

"We sent no note. Come sit with me. We need to figure this out. If you go racing off, you might fall into enemy hands." Corona took Valeria's hand.

By "enemy," Corona had to mean their family, more specifically, Isabella. But if they were involved, the note would imply that Isabella knew where both sisters were and had not attacked. What reason would she have for not attacking? Probably only if the sisters still being alive was useful to the demon matriarch. The overwhelming amount of power that ended up in her special spell circle came to mind.

"What do you suggest?" Valeria helped Corona to the rocking chair.

"You told me about how you found me and the golden magic. Can you do that again?" Corona sat with a sigh.

The day Valeria had discovered her dawn magic, she had set up her spell circle and gone into a trance. Could she do that magic without her circle? Even with the tattoos, her body could still be harmed when she spirit walked. "You will watch over me?"

"Always." Corona pulled out a wand. Her husband must have given the device to her.

Valeria had to try. The feeling that time was running out increased with each beat of her heart. She relaxed and fell into a trance. Her mind drifted to an image of future Corona. She was just as heavily pregnant. Her stomach rippled in a contraction. A dark swirling vortex of energy hovered above her. The energy sat poised to attack the babe.

Why was she being shown this image?

Corona flung her hand out, and a small swirl of power hit the vortex squarely. The dark magic shivered and extended, forming a long thin tail that stretched away.

The future Corona gazed directly at Valeria. "Follow the tails."

Valeria used her spirit form to follow the long, thin thread. The world around her fuzzed and changed. She got the sense she was not just moving in space but in time.

The background changed so she could see some of the buildings. She recognized the street she was on. This one led to the building in the center of Old Town where her family held ceremonies. This was a place she had never seen again after she had left the family. Gutted buildings leaned away from the wooden two-story building. The magical tail led within the door and probably down to the basement.

Valeria had no urge to advance into that basement ever again. Although she might be able to win a fight against an aunt or two, Isabella was far stronger than Valeria. Valeria was not strong enough to defeat her whole family, especially in their home base.

She must be here for a reason. Did the tail represent a link or causation between her family and events they had caused? Perhaps when Corona had said "follow the tails" she meant one of the other threads that lead away from the basement. Was this vision meant to reveal the interconnectedness she had been missing?

There were too many other threads to follow from the basement. One or two of them must be important. When she reached for her power, the faint tinkling of bells and the smell of fresh bread heralded the golden energy coursing within her.

The magic coalesced into a ball that hesitated between three tails. One she could tell led far out of the city to the east. She left that one alone. The next two should lead to closer events.

Did the threads represent Isabella's schemes within this world? If so, to what end?

She followed the darkest of the threads away from the casting house and down the road. As she followed, floating along, the air shimmered, and she recognized a street in New Nadezhda. In the vision, she was back in the real world. Alex had been right to suspect that there was a crack open between the two worlds.

The tail headed just out of the city to a town surrounded by a shimmering bubble. This must be Hope, the town that Max and Rose were from. The trees around the bubble were much smaller, leaving the impression that this vision was from a long time ago.

A man who could be a younger version of the mage Rose had tackled into Valeria's magic circle stepped into the clearing. A younger, softer-looking Isabella gave him a necklace. Valeria didn't dare get any closer to Isabella. Even though Isabella shouldn't be able to sense her, Valeria was taking no chances. The man left quickly. A few minutes later, another young man, who looked like he was related to the first, also accepted a necklace. The second necklace looked to be the one Rose had been wearing.

Did that mean Isabella was not only responsible for the control elements that both Rose and Max had, but had plotted to add the extra magical power the mages had? Valeria remembered Wren saying that the power from the shield went into the necklaces. That power would have been enough to open the way to the Abyss. Isabella's scheming was at the root of this plot.

The other thread called to her. She would prefer not to go

back to the ceremony house unless she had to. The golden glow could find the other thread.

That thread led away, and she felt herself sink through time. Newly toppled buildings, chaotic magic, rising smoke, and the confused, fearful interactions of the people made her wonder if she was seeing New Nadezhda directly after the Merge. The town was in shambles.

The thread led her north of town to a brightly colored phoenix with intelligent eyes trapped in a black net. A dozen demons held down the ends. Isabella unsheathed a flaming black sword and plunged the blade into the phoenix's chest. The phoenix's flames rose. Isabella jumped back to safety, but the rest of the demons and the net caught fire and burned.

"Run while you can, phoenix. I win either way. If you can't be reborn, the crack that leads to the Abyss will get bigger until the worlds merge. If you do get reborn, I will use your power to merge this new world and the Abyss." Isabella laughed, a long, loud laugh that sent shivers through Valeria.

The phoenix screamed and launched into the air. The thread followed, pulling Valeria to a nest that sat in the middle of a rocky slope. The same phoenix from earlier shivered in the nest. The black line of magic impaled the phoenix's chest where Isabella had used the sword. The phoenix closed her eyes, and the bright colors leached from her feathers, leaving them a dull gray. Blood dripped down from her wound.

Valeria let out a bit of magic. The phoenix was dying. The demon magic appeared to be corrupting the phoenix's magic and stealing her power. The sword must have been cursed. The phoenix seemed moments away from dying forever. This was a vision, and nothing Valeria did would affect the outcome. She hated how helpless she felt by that fact.

Six Aeros fluttered down from the sky. Four had drawn

swords, and two radiated magic. One pregnant female with a striking resemblance to Alesia hunched near the phoenix.

"She's still alive," the woman said.

The man next to her raised a hand and bright silver magic coated them all. "The demons have attached to her life force. The next time she dies, they are going to steal her energy."

"What would they do with such power?" The woman reached down and placed a hand on the phoenix's chest. The soft glow of magic filled the space.

The phoenix raised her head and iridescent eyes sparkled back. "They will rip open the portal to the Abyss and allow all of the creatures of hell to live here."

The man put his hand on the woman's shoulder. His face was dirty and pale. "What can we do to break the spell?"

"The spell is complex. I cannot break it. Only one of her bloodline can."

"Then what can we do?" The man helped the woman stand.

The woman gasped and then closed her eyes, placing her hand on her stomach. The woman glowed with divination magic for a moment.

"You had a vision." The man's mouth pressed into a grim line.

"We must sacrifice, or this world will be overrun by demons and die." Tears streaked down the woman's cheeks, making trails through the dirt.

The man bowed his head. "Then we do what we must."

"We can delay." The woman took the man's hands. "If we separate the parts of the phoenix, we can combine her fire and spirit into our unborn children. The souls will combine and offer the phoenix safe harbor."

"What will happen to our children?"

The phoenix's eyes flashed, and divination magic shimmered. "Two halves united shall burn and be reborn."

The golden ball bobbled and led Valeria away before she could witness the magic. The way back through the devastated city allowed her to appreciate how far the citizens had come. The city and its people were not perfect, but they had individuals willing to stand up and protect the innocent.

Valeria's magic brought her back to herself. Her body still sat next to Corona.

"What did you see?" Corona handed her a teacup of water.

Valeria took a small sip, letting the cool water calm her. She told Corona about Rose and Max. "Isabella was not only behind the magic controlling Rose and Max, but she also cursed a phoenix so when the phoenix is reborn, its rebirth will break open the Abyss."

"What?" Corona clutched her hand. "If you think the aunts are powerful now, if they have free access to our world, there would be no stopping them. William!"

"The spell can only be broken by one of her blood." Valeria repeated what Wren's ancestor had said.

An alarm sounded through the house.

Corona clutched Valeria's hand "You. You must break the spell. Is that why you were tricked into coming here? So you won't be able to help them?"

"Corona!" William ran in, grabbing Corona's arm. "The demons are coming. Come, we must go to the safe room." He helped Corona stand. "Valeria, we can keep you safe."

Valeria stood. "No. This is the distraction. Wren is in trouble." The world was in trouble.

Corona resisted her husband's pull. She reached into her pocket. "Take this. You will need the charm more than the baby will right now."

Valeria stepped close, memorizing her sister's expression. She might never see her again.

Corona put the charm around Valeria's neck. "I believe in you."

Valeria kissed her sister's cheek and patted her tummy. Fear soured her stomach, but what choice did she have but to fight?

William all but lifted Corona away to safety. The shouts of his brothers came from deeper in the house. A shriek of a demon preparing for battle rattled the windows.

Valeria slipped out the door into the darkness, praying to her Goddess that she was not too late.

20

WREN

<u>Wee Hours, Primum third, 300 years post-Merge</u>

Wren opened his eyes and wished he hadn't. The pain in his head was nothing compared to the pain that stabbed his heart at the view of Alesia's prone form. Transparent flames flickered around her, and a golden glow surrounded her body. His breath caught in his throat. What was going on?

"Alesia?" He struggled to sit. The room spun and he leaned back.

Blackie whined and nudged Alesia, licking her face. She moved, patted the dog, and slowly sat up.

Wren let out a sigh of relief. She seemed to be alright.

The dog wiggled onto her lap. A charm hung off the dog's collar that radiated a faint golden glow.

"I'm not dead. Not yet anyway." Alesia brought the hand not petting the dog to her head.

They both turned to gaze at Wren. Blackie growled, and Alesia gasped. "No."

"What's wrong?" Wren reached for his sister. His hand was not only transparent, but the same black ooze that had surrounded Rose and Max coated his hand. He looked down at his body. He was transparent and covered in the black sludge. "What happened to us?"

Alesia stood and backed a step away from him.

The sound of sobbing drew his gaze. The flickering flames bathed the rest of the room except in a protected area that must have been where the spell circle was. Rye sat slumped in the center, crying.

"We are in our spirit forms." Alesia backed another step until she was pressed against the wall. Her face was an emotionless mask, but her eyes begged him for something.

Wren's heart thudded in his chest. Being in the spirit form meant they were dead. Who knew he could feel the same in his spirit form? He killed the demon who had possessed the dog, but he still had that unnatural urge to see his sister. The bubbling magic probably meant the demons wanted him to reunite with his sister for some reason. No, not for some reason but because of the prophecy.

Son and daughter of the saviors of fenix
Time runs out to repair
that which was sundered after the Merge
Isolate the pair until first light on her day of birth
Seek the kept flame and release
Two halves united shall burn and be reborn
Only a bound witch can save them all
Or the immortal shall die
and break open fully the portal to the Abyss.

. . .

Phoenixes were so prevalent in the Rookery that Valeria thought they were a house emblem. Wren had fire magic that he got from his grand-uncle. That could cover the burn, but the "reborn'" didn't make sense unless the intelligence that possessed Alesia was from the phoenix. So if Wren and Alesia reunited, that would reunite the phoenix, which would trigger what phoenixes were known for. The bird would set fire to itself to be reborn. How did *the immortal shall die* part fit in?

Maybe the demon magic would cause the phoenix to die this time. He could see proof of the demons' interference in his own aura here on the spirit plane, where the magic had probably hidden.

Blackie had shown up at odd places and had been very un-dog-like. Could he have been the reason his door was open and Valeria had caught him sleepwalking? Blackie was even the cause of the fire removal spell failing and had tricked him into the phoenix room with Alesia.

"How did they get you?" Wren's throat was so tight, his voice was barely a whisper.

"I woke up outside of Walter's burrows. Five women grabbed me. I saw the Rookery delivery bag before they knocked me out." Her gaze traveled over Wren's body. She frowned and bit her lip the way she did when she was worried.

The black ooze around him thickened, and that itch he had been fighting strengthened. "What's going on?"

"Demons are exerting their control on you," Alesia said. "You must fight."

The urge to walk over to his sister and give her a hug increased. The feeling became like ants crawling up his body. "The demons want me to touch you, Alesia."

"Not yet. You need to resist. We need the witch." Alesia's voice grew soft and coaxing.

Wren stood on shaking legs. The act lessened the itch. Looking at Alesia lessened the itch even more. Taking a step closer should as well. He took a half step closer for some relief.

Blackie jumped between Wren and Alesia. The dog barked and snapped at Wren, forcing him to take a step back. The charm on the dog's collar glowed brighter, surrounding the dog in golden light. Blackie growled, and the hair on his back stood up, making him look much bigger but not at all like the demon who had possessed him.

Wren tried to slide to the side of the room, but Blackie turned to keep him away from Alesia.

Was there anything he could do to lessen the itch? He reached for his magic but couldn't find the power. Everything was muted as if he had no magic. He had never practiced spells in the spirit world, and he was far too emotional for any spell to work well. How could he break the demon's control? Could he use witchcraft?

The dozen ants turned into a hundred and then a thousand. He backed away. The feeling intensified and brought him to his knees. He whimpered in pain and fear.

"Wren?" Alesia's voice was high-pitched and unsteady.

If he didn't give in to the call, then Alesia would come to him to try and help with his pain.

"Don't," he choked out, scrambling back even though that action increased the torment.

Wren was not sure how long he could resist and give Valeria a chance to save them.

21

VALERIA

<u>Wee Hours, Primum third, 300 years post-Merge</u>

Valeria cast her only spell to fly as soon as she exited the house and hit Corona's courtyard.

Pain slashed her chest. The feeling that she was too late and Wren was already dead filled her with dread. No, she was not going to believe it was too late. Not until she saw a body.

The trip across town seemed to take forever even with flying. The Rookery shone in the darkness. Every light on every floor glowed. She ignored the shouts as she flew into the Rookery and merged into the aerial traffic. Soaring past startled Aeros and other birds would be much more fun if she wasn't so worried. Where would Wren be?

A distressed male cry came from the same floor as the phoenix room. She flew to that level and down the hall. Pounding on the door was a Lizardfolk with his red dewlap extended from his throat in distress. The only Lizardfolk who might visit here was Wren's best friend and Alesia's protector, Walter.

"Walter?" Valeria asked as she released the fly spell and caught her balance.

His tail whipped as he turned toward her. "You musssssst be the witch."

She blinked in surprise. "I must be?"

"Alesia snuck out and left me this note." He handed Valeria a scrap of paper.

It's time.

Aid the witch who finds you. She must break the demon's hold.

No matter what happens, know we have a bond of love.

A

When Valeria had finished reading the writing, Walter snatched the paper back. He carefully tucked the note in his pocket.

"How did you know to come here?"

Walter flicked his eye membranes shut, and his tail lashed. "Alesssssia getsssss losssssst in the visionsssssss. I have a ssssspell that allowsssss me to find her."

"That is good." She chanced to put her hand on his arm. They needed to be on the same side. "So she is in this room?"

Walter nodded. "The door is locked."

"I–" What she was going to say was lost when the lock clicked and the door opened.

Rye peered out. Soot covered her face except for the clean spots under both her eyes and cheeks provided by her tears and from around her temples created by sweat. "You have to help them."

Valeria pushed into the room and froze in shock. Two charred bodies lay to the side of the still glowing protective circle. The flames crackled and rolled, reaching the ceiling and blackening the stone. Rye must have been in the circle to survive the heat.

"Are you sure Alesia was here?" Valeria's voice came out as a croak. She could just make out wings on both sets of remains.

Valeria was too late.

Grief pushed her to her knees. No way anyone had survived the fire, even with fire charms and protections. Without using magic sight, she could feel the power and magic embedded in the flames.

Walter pulled Valeria into his chest. Even as he shook, his voice murmured in her ear, "Itssss not your fault."

Rye grabbed a hold of Valeria and sobbed. "I couldn't stop her. I'm so sorry."

The girl blurred with a blink, which explained the hot feel of Valeria's eyes. The heaviness of her chest made breathing hard.

The ache in her sternum grew. Walter shook in her arms, just as upset as she was. Rye sounded like she had lost everything in the world.

Yes, the blame laid on Isabella for creating the situation, but if only Valeria would have been here. She could have helped. According to the prophecy, she could have saved them.

The words of the prophecy calmed her. They repeated in her head.

Son and daughter of the saviors of fenix

Time runs out to repair
that which was sundered after the Merge
Isolate the pair until first light on her day of birth
Seek the kept flame and release
Two halves united shall burn and be reborn
Only a bound witch can save them all
Or the immortal shall die
and break open fully the portal to the Abyss.

The two halves had reunited and burned, but they had not been reborn yet. She pulled away from Walter and wiped her eyes. The nest stood empty. Was that a good sign that she still had time to at least free the phoenix? She needed more information.

Valeria knelt and took Rye's tear-streaked face in her hands. "Tell me what happened."

"I'm sorry for tricking you." The girl sobbed.

Valeria rubbed her back. "Please. What happened here?"

The girl hiccupped and took a breath. "The demon got into my dog. The mean women said if I didn't help, they would kill him. We have been together for so long, and he saved my life..." The girl started sobbing again.

"How did you trick me?" An idea was beginning to form that her grandmother had been even more involved than she had been expecting.

"I was the one who sent the note from the Archive. The demon told me what to write."

"What else did you do?"

"I tricked Wren into this room and locked the door. The demon said his own control element would force him to his sister's side."

Valeria still felt as if she were missing something. "How did Alesia get here?"

"I don't know." Rye shook in Valeria's arms.

"Tell me what you know."

Rye told them about Wren fighting the demon-dog, Alesia passing through the spell lines without the spell breaking, and about the flames rising.

Rage and grief had her shaking. What was she going to do?

"Why is there still so much magic?" Rye asked.

Her words penetrated Valeria's grief.

"The flamesssss aren't getting any sssssmaller," Walter said.

Valeria looked up again. The power was there as if the magic was waiting on something.

She thought about everything she knew and still had no idea what to do. Everything Wren and she had practiced had been about breaking control elements and about redirecting the energy.

"What do we do?" Walter asked. "The flame issss sssssstarting to affect the roof. If it getsssss out of thissss room, it could take down the whole tower."

Valeria stepped back, her mind shifting through spells. She could get the flames out if she did a big enough cold spell. That was not the answer.

She let out her magical senses. A sense of yearning filled the space. That same feeling when she had first seen the Meeps. Somehow, the parts of the phoenix had not yet reunited.

Perhaps she needed to do that same spell to bring the parts of the phoenix together. But the vision from Corona's house showed that the phoenix had the same issue that Rose and Max had. The demons had possession of the phoenix.

Suddenly the picture made sense. The control element must have gone with the fire and lived within Wren. That was the cause of his almost overwhelming desire to see his sister. If the phoenix had not yet been merged, then the battle must be taking place on the spirit realm. Wren's and Alesia's spirits must still be in the room. Perhaps, as the note said, the bond of love between Walter and Alesia was keeping Alesia here, but what would keep Wren?

Only a bound witch can save them all

Valeria was a witch, but was she bound? She checked her own aura and realized that she had a connection that led to Wren. That explained why she could exchange magic with him so easily and why she had felt when he had died. She was lucky she was a witch, or she would have died at the same time. Perhaps when she had been healing his soul and adding back the pieces, the bond had occurred.

The whens didn't matter. Part of her own energy kept Wren close but in the spirit realm, which raised the stakes even more. If she was not able to save Wren, she would die as well. That would leave her sister even more vulnerable. She pushed away the fear. She needed to focus her energy on solving her problem.

The end battle had to happen in the spirit realm. Valeria would have to break that demon control and then bring the phoenix parts together. She'd worry about the rest of the prophecy later.

Intuition had her grab Walter's shoulder. "Walter? Pull out the spell you have for finding Alesia."

"Of courssssssss." He went into his pocket and took out a small rose.

"No matter what happens, protect me." Valeria held Walter's gaze and then Rye's until they both nodded.

Valeria sat back in the hallway that led into the phoenix room. There was no time to set up her personal circle, and it was too dangerous to use the spell circle from within the room. She sent a prayer to the Goddess that she was doing the right thing.

Focusing on the baked-bread smell and the ringing of bells,

she pooled her magic. Once she had enough power, she entered into the spirit world.

Cloaked in the same black ooze, Wren stood with his back toward her. The spell circle was situated to her right. The dog, Blackie, stood between him and Alesia. The dog glowed with a golden light coming from the charm on his collar. He growled and snapped at Wren, keeping him away from Alesia.

"Wren?"

He didn't respond. Had the possession gone to the final level? Valeria needed his attention. She pulled the bond she had with Wren, and he turned toward her.

His face twisted into an ugly sneer. "You can't keep me away from my sister, witch."

Valeria swallowed her nerves. "What are you going to do? You can't do magic in this place."

Wren's face twisted even more. The demon itself might be able to do magic here. Isabella had been able to. At least Wren's own magic would be inaccessible. She thought about everything she knew about demons. Ego was one of their biggest flaws.

"I bet you got old and powerless being stuck inside the Aeros and made to sleep for all those years," Valeria taunted.

Wren growled low and turned to face her fully. "You think you're so smart."

"No, I think you are so weak. I already took out one of your kind in my life. A level-six one to be exact." Valeria tried to project arrogance in her tone. She needed to get the demon away from Alesia.

Wren hesitated and pulled on his lip, a move Valeria had never seen Wren do. Another indication that Wren had been fully possessed. She had no idea what the timeline was before the demon won. Wren's and Alesia's bodies were no longer usable. The fire would have destroyed them passed reviving.

Valeria had no attack magic. A creature from the Abyss

usually did. She could not run and hide, because the demon would figure out how to get past the charm that Blackie wore. She sent a prayer of thanks to the Goddess that Rye had been smart enough to attach the charm to the dog's collar.

The only item within the room was the embedded circle. The circle that had been here when they'd first seen the room. Valeria's intuition said that was an important fact. She slid along the wall to be closer to the ring.

This room had been built by Wren's grandmother, who had also set up the way to regain power in the Archive and keyed that into being a witch. The woman had sent message after message for them in the things she had left behind. She must have been a strong diviner, or she would not have been able to do so. The fact that her twin with the fire also had demon influence explained why she could not trust her messages out in the open. So all actions and messages had to be subtle.

Trusting that this circle would solve her issues was a leap of faith. If she was wrong, then she may add to the demon's power, but if she was right, then the circle would help her trap the demonic influence. The ring could act like a container, the same way that Corona and her husband had helped Valeria pull away her own demon. At least Wren probably didn't have to kill what possessed him since they were not born in the same body.

Now all she had to do was get Wren and the demon inside the circle and activate the protective energies. Hopefully that would break the possession.. Getting Wren out of the ring would be her next task. She had no idea how to make that happen. She'd have to improvise.

Valeria backed to the wall, edged so she was on the circle's far side, and then smiled at the demon. She worked to school her expression to mimic the way Wren looked as his default, with a slightly contemptuous air. "You are, what? A level two-demon?" She even tried to add a sneer to her voice as she readied herself to add power to the spell.

The widening of Wren's nostrils and the narrowing of his eyes said the barb hit its mark. He gritted his teeth and hissed.

"If only you were a real challenge." She smirked at the demon who took a half step forward in response. He was so close to the edge of the ring.

"I am stronger than you, little witch." The demon huffed and took another step forward.

Valeria pretended to lean back against the wall of the chamber and then widened her arms. She snorted. "Sure, come and get me."

The demon snarled and leapt forward, right into the middle of the spell.

She slapped power into the spell, and the demon roared. The black ichor rose out of Wren with another unearthly cry. She ran around the circle trying to get at Wren, but the demon streaked toward her new position. He bashed against the spell circle and shrieked. No matter what side she ran to, the demon met her there. Every time the demon touched the ring, a small lick of flame kicked up. Normal protection spells did not have fire. What was causing that?

Valeria reached out to feel the magic. Protection against demons was there, but also embedded in the ring was a spell to create an inferno.

Out of the corner of her eye, she saw Blackie step into the circle. She froze. Had Wren's grandmother created the spell circle to account for people entering and leaving it? If the dog crossing the boundary shut off the spell, they would all be doomed.

Valeria held her breath while the dog's golden glow merged with the spell circle's. The spell stayed intact. Did that mean any intrusion was fine? Or just the dog because of the charm? The demon slammed into the barrier near her face. She jumped back in surprise. Her heart raced.

She raised her hands as if she were casting a spell. He dodged back.

This demon didn't know much about witches, or he would know that she was not able to attack him. Offensive magic went against the nature of most witches.

Alesia came to her side. "Demon, what do you want?" Her voice shook, but the golden glow around her stayed steady.

She must be trying to help Valeria distract the demon.

"There is still time to come to the winning side," he said, hovering closer. "I could take away your pain and make life so much easier for you." The demon purred the last sentence.

Alesia hesitated. Her smile was uncertain. She closed her eyes as if imagining her life without a care.

The demon shifted closer. "I just need you to lower the barrier."

Across the circle, Blackie grabbed Wren's collar and dragged him out. Or at least he tried to. Blackie was not strong enough to pull Wren. Even if Blackie could pull Wren out, would Wren be able to leave the spell without breaking the magic?

"Alesia, no. The demon will not actually help you." Valeria searched through the reasons she could use. Maybe that Alesia no longer had a body anyway and she was most likely dead. No, that would just remind him that they were in the spirit realm. She could remind Alesia that her brother needed her. But that would bring the demon's attention back to Wren, who was currently being unsuccessfully dragged away.

"Aww...little one. I can help keep you *and* your brother safe." The demon's voice was low and soft as if he were talking to a friend.

"You are too weak to help her," Valeria said, deciding that taunting might be the most effective distraction.

He sneered at her. "I am very powerful, little witch. Do you think Isabella would send someone weak to deal with the phoenix?" He put a more pleasant expression on his face and made his face morph to look more like Alesia's brother. "Come, sweetie, I can help you if you help me."

Alesia raised her hand as if she would touch the demon and thereby break the spell. Maybe? "Will you keep us safe?"

"Oh, little one, I would make sure that you were rewarded." The demon all but beamed at Alesia.

"Alesia, it's a trick," Valeria said. How could Alesia not know that?

"Get away from me." Alesia put her back toward the demon. She smiled and winked, before pushing Valeria hard against the wall. She flew through the wall and out of the tower. The city spread out below her, but nothing else flew in the sky.

Valeria screamed and fell a few floors before she remembered she was in the spirit realm. She could fly here with no effort or spell.

She hovered a few feet from the ground and panted, trying to get her heart under control. Why had Alesia done that? She would have known that pushing Valeria out of the wall would not harm her. All it did was stop Valeria from seeing what was going on. Which meant the demon couldn't see Valeria either. Why would Alesia do that unless it was to help Wren?

Maybe Valeria could circle around and get Wren out of the spell. But how was she going to hide from the demon? Even before entering the room, he would know that she was there. How would she prevent the demon from detecting her?

The charm that Corona gave back. The whole purpose of the charm was to hide from demons. Valeria dug out the charm and activated it. Hopefully the charm would work in this world.

She went around the tower and entered the far side through a window on the right level. The room's door led into the hallway. Walter paced up and down the hall that led to the phoenix room with his tail lashing and dewlap extended. Valeria's body remained slumped against the wall. Rye leaned against the same wall.

"It'sssss been too long. We need to go in there," Walter muttered.

"Please no, not yet, they need more time." Rye jumped up and grabbed his arm.

Valeria floated past them and into the room. The demon was on the far side of the circle farthest away from where the dog struggled to pull Wren out. Valeria took a deep breath and hoped she would be able to enter without disrupting the spell. She didn't understand the rules, which made her uneasy.

She entered the circle and sagged for a moment when the magic held. She pushed Blackie off Wren and grabbed him under his armpits. Wren didn't move at all when she pulled.

She stumbled and grunted. Wren was super heavy.

"What are you doing?" The demon turned toward her.

Blackie growled and rushed forward to attack. The dog howled before he grabbed the demon's leg and bit down.

Valeria hesitated. The dog was in danger, but unless she got Wren out of the spell, the demon could just take him over again. She pulled and struggled until Wren's heavy body was outside of the line. She could feel the magic snap shut behind her.

The dog yelped, drawing her attention back to the demon and the dog. He had his claws around the dog as the dog squirmed and fought to get away.

"Compress the circle!" Alesia yelled.

Valeria pushed power into the spell and contracted the ring. The dog whimpered. She needed to hurry so she could save the dog's spirit.

The magic got smaller. The golden light touched the demon and it shrieked, letting go of the dog. The dog fell in a heap.

Valeria used her power to lift the spell off the ground, which left the dog under the sphere.

Her own magic flagged. She would just have enough energy to activate the inferno spell, but she would not be able to help bring the phoenix together.

She fell to her knees and closed her eyes to focus the last of her power. The world grayed around her as the ring slowly contracted and the fire spell activated. If she didn't have enough power, she had no idea what would happen. Would the circle expand? Or would the circle break when she passed out and fell unconscious? Would the inferno escape the barrier?

Sparkles danced in her vision. She slumped back to the floor, keeping her power as steady as she could. The spell was only a few inches apart with flames so hot they were blue. Would it be enough to destroy the demon?

She closed her eyes and with the last of her power, she pushed everything she had into closing that ring and feeding the flames.

Blackie barked loudly as she passed out. Did she fail?

22

WREN

Dawn, Primum third, 300 years post-Merge

The barking near his head woke Wren. Damn, what was Blackie getting into now?

He opened his eyes and wasn't sure what he was seeing. Blackie and Alesia sat near him on a stone floor. They both glowed with a bright golden light. He lifted his own hand, which did not have such a glow, but it was also not covered in ooze.

"What happened?"

Blackie came and licked his face.

"The witch cast out the demon and went back to the real world." Alesia grimaced. "Yes, this is a real world, too, but just for spirits." The last was said as if she were conversing with someone else who had just corrected her.

"Who are you talking to?" Wren sat up. The room spun, and his head throbbed. Why did the spirit realm still have headaches? He had no body.

"I feel like I drank too much."

Alesia slid closer and touched his arm. "I'm talking to the phoenix."

Wren looked up at a noise. The door banged open, and Walter and Rye stormed into the room. He could see the edge of Valeria in the hall. Was she unconscious?

"You can do that?" Wren leaned his head on his sister's shoulder, which was a move he had not done since they were little.

"In this realm, yes."

"What are we going to do next?" Wren rubbed his head, which did nothing to dispel how badly he felt. His hands produced flames as he rubbed. "I held the phoenix's fire, and you held her spirit."

"Yes."

"I no longer feel the pull to touch you."

"That's the witch's doing. She broke the demon's hold." Alesia watched Walter. Her eyes were sad.

Wren stood up. His sister looked like she had been through a lot. Her hair was a mess, flying every direction. Even some of her feathers looked as if they needed to be groomed. She had a bruise on one cheek and seemed very pale, but thankfully she appeared to have no other injuries. He was sure by the worry in her gaze he looked just as bad if not worse. He leaned over and then hugged his sister.

"I am so glad to see you again. I was not sure I was ever going to be able to." Mixed feelings accompanied those words. He was elated to be in her company again, but they had lost. Their bodies were no more, and soon the pull to move to the next world would descend.

She hugged him back hard.

"I missed you." She pulled back and her eyes were now the shimmer of the phoenix. "All is not lost yet."

Wren remembered back to the Meeps. The way the

atmosphere changed just before they merged into the egg. This room felt the same way. His mage magic would not work here, but maybe he could try to cast a spell as a witch. A tether stretched back to Valeria. He couldn't perceive anything on the other side.

She said that witches used their emotions to feed the spell. He had plenty of those churning in his chest and stomach.

He closed his eyes again and embraced how thankful he was that he had met Valeria. How attracted he was to her. He wanted to see if she had similar feelings. He needed to protect the world some more. How good hugging his sister felt and how happy he was that she had found love with Walter. The sadness followed that their love would end so soon after they had found it. He was even grateful to that damn dog because he helped with the phoenix. His chest grew heavy, and his eyes stung.

He funneled the emotions into what he remembered Valeria doing with the Meeps. Magic flowed around him. Heat pulled on the surface of his skin, and he could feel Alesia shaking in his arms. There was not enough power.

Wren let himself truly feel his protective instincts toward the ragtag group of people he had helped earlier. Joshua and Serene were so frustrating and yet so good. Rose and Max, who were caught in a web of another's creation. They all had been there for him when he needed them. But mostly he thought of Valeria. He focused his attention toward her and the admiration he had for who she was. The joy that filled his chest with warmth that he might have a chance to see if the attraction was mutual and if they would, in fact, make a good couple.

The last emotion tightened his chest. With a clap of force, Wren flew through the air and landed on his butt on the floor. Alesia sat next to him looking as startled as he felt. The golden glow swirled together until the power merged with another clap of force. When the smoke cleared, a large phoenix with dulled feathers and a seeping chest wound sprawled on the stone. The phoenix gave a low sound of both triumph and pain.

"You have freed me in time." The phoenix's feminine voice was in Wren's head. "I will grant you a boon."

"Bring back Blackie." Then Rye would have her protector. Wren had a feeling he owed that damn dog for saving his life. The dog in question barked and licked his face.

"Ugh, get off me, you mangy mutt." Wren scratched the dog instead of pushing him away.

The phoenix laughed in his head. "As you wish."

The phoenix went over to where the charred remains were and settled inside of the still flaming bodies.

A flash of light was the last thing Wren saw before darkness claimed him.

23

VALERIA

<u>Just after Dawn, Primum third, 300 years post-Merge</u>

The rush of power woke Valeria. She blinked her eyes open to see the ceiling. She was alive, and a rush of joy filled her. She slowly sat up.

"Valeria!" Rye squealed and landed on her lap. She hugged Valeria. "I thought you were dead too." The girl burst into tears.

Valeria rubbed her back and looked around. Past the open doorway, the remains still burned in the middle of the room. That part had not changed. Wren and Alesia were still dead. Valeria's chest ached, making it hard to breathe. The room spun and her vision blurred.

Walter stood by the burning bodies. His tail swished back and forth.

"What happened?" Valeria croaked.

"You collapsed and the room quaked and everyone was gone." Rye shook in her arms.

Valeria tried to extend her magical sense, but she had no

energy. Even without her magic, the feeling of the room changed.

"What's going on?" Valeria asked.

"There'sssss an egg," Walter said.

Valeria and Rye stood and hurried to where Walter stood by the fire. As the flames subsided, the egg grew. The flames spluttered out. The red and gold egg throbbed and pulsed until with a flash of power, the egg cracked open.

A fiery chick spilled out of the egg and chirped. The phoenix shook itself. "The crack to the Abyss is sealed." A female voice thrummed through the air.

Valeria sagged. If nothing else, that should cut Isabella's power. "Where are Wren and Alesia's spirits?"

The phoenix cocked her head to the side. "If I had the energy, I could regenerate them."

Valeria realized that she still had the amulets with all the extra power from the encounter with Rose and the evil mages. She pulled the amulets out and offered them to the phoenix. "Here. Use these."

"These are very formidable. You could rule the city."

Valeria didn't even have to think about her answer. "Save Wren and Alesia."

The phoenix nodded and closed her eyes. The two amulets faded as the ashes around the phoenix swirled and funneled into two columns. The ashes swirled and the light intensified. A pop of bright light blinded Valeria.

When her sight cleared, Wren and Alesia stood, blinking.

Valeria's chest lightened.

"Wren?" Valeria swallowed hard at the lump in her throat. She threw herself at Wren and hugged him. Rye was next to Valeria, hitting Wren and knocking them both over.

"Alesssia?" Walter ran to her and hugged her close.

"You are alive. I'm glad you are safe," Wren murmured in her hair and hugged her tighter.

A dog barked. Blackie joined the hug pile and landed on Rye's lap.

"You saved my dog!" Tears fell down Rye's face, and she rubbed them into the dog's fur.

Wren laughed. "I thought you might need him."

"I'm sorry for everything. I understand if I need to leave." Rye backed away and hiccupped, wiping her eyes as she moved.

Wren helped Valeria stand and kept his arm around her, making her chest warm with affection.

"You should stay, but the choice is yours." Wren ruffled Rye's hair.

"I want to stay, but can Blackie stay? He no longer has a demon so he-will-be-much-better-behaved." Rye talked so fast the last part came out together.

Wren snorted as if he knew she was lying. "I don't believe that for a second."

Rye's face fell, and her lower lip trembled.

"He's still allowed to stay," Wren said.

Valeria squeezed Wren's waist gently. He really was so soft inside.

"Wren, you owe me." Walter stood back, his tail held stiff, meaning he was not sure of his reception.

Wren released Valeria and hugged Walter.

"Almosssst dying makesss you ssssappy," Walter groused, but he hugged him back. Valeria could see Walter shaking.

"Thank you, my friend, for keeping my sister safe."

Walter pulled back and tilted his head. His dewlap fluttered. "I wish to marry your sister."

Alesia gasped.

"You have my blessing if she wishes to do so," Wren said.

Walter released Wren and hugged Alesia, spinning her

around and kissing her. Alesia's delighted giggles warmed Valeria's heart.

"I need to check on my sister and let her know the good news." Valeria leaned against the wall. Once she fell asleep, she would sleep for a week.

"Let's all go."

"Wait." Alesia bowed to the phoenix "Thank you. For everything."

The phoenix chuckled. "It is you and your ancestors who saved me from the demons."

"It was our honor to help." Wren also bowed.

"Until we meet again." The phoenix gave a sharp cry and shot up into the sky.

Wren picked Valeria up and followed.

Not too long later, Corona's home came into view. Wren set Valeria down gently. Alesia landed next with Walter holding on. The poor man looked pale and wide-eyed. A guard deposited Rye and Blackie before taking off for the roof.

The phoenix circled once before streaking away.

Valeria hurried down the sidewalk to Corona's house. Black scorch marks dotted the siding. The shutters were off, and broken glass littered the yard. The wooden door opened at a touch. The shimmer of magic made her feel slightly better about the automatically opening door.

"What happened here?" Wren followed her.

"The demons attacked after I was tricked into coming here." Valeria glanced around the entryway. The same wallpapered walls and carpet greeted her. There was no damage inside. Maybe the demons had not breached the house's defenses.

"Sorry," Rye said in a squeaky tone.

Valeria patted her shoulder. "You did what you had to and kept your word to tell me who was hurting you as soon as you could."

Wren's head whipped around. "Who was...the demon."

Rye nodded.

"I should have noticed." Wren's head feathers rose.

"I made sure you didn't."

Valeria understood how Wren felt. The demons had aided in them not knowing that Rye was suffering. "Did you mean to wake me up that night?" The dining area was empty and clear of demon signs.

"No, but I was hoping if you stayed in the hall you would hear Wren come down the stairs."

"Good thinking." Valeria ruffled Rye's hair.

Alesia and Walter walked through the door at the far end of the dining hall. "The building is empty."

"Corona!" Valeria yelled. "I have news." She moved from room to room shouting the same thing.

A creak off the dining room drew her attention. "Corona?"

A pale-faced William and his five brothers stormed out of the hidden door with magic wands out.

"Valeria, it *is* you. Who are your friends? What news do you have? You need to come quickly." William's frantic phrases almost made no sense. He wrung his hands and fidgeted. What was wrong with him?

"We think the Abyss is closed, and the family curse is broken. I'm just here in case we are wrong," Valeria said.

William blinked and then grabbed her hand. "Come with me."

He dragged her through the door and down some stairs into what had to be a casting room. A large, comfy couch sat in the middle of the etched spell circle. The homey atmosphere made Valeria smile. Corona reclined on the couch fast asleep. Even the kick of the baby was not enough to wake her up.

A contraction rippled through her belly.

"The baby is coming." A woman in black who had a kind face stepped closer to Corona.

Valeria nodded. "I need to make sure the demons don't..."

"Are you sure this is wise?" Wren was next to her. "Do you have enough energy to check?"

"Probably just barely. Will you keep me safe?"

Wren swallowed. "Always."

Valeria sat with the spell circle. She meditated and got into her spirit form. Once she was there, she searched for signs of possession. Corona watched her from the couch. Her aura was like pure sunshine with no hint of demonic influence on her sister or the baby.

The magic came slowly to her call. She let the baked bread and the tinkling of bells soothe her until she had enough power to create the golden globe. She sought the threads that she had looked at earlier. She wanted confirmation that the crack to the demon realm was closed, and Isabella was gone.

Valeria followed the ball to the road that led to the family's basement. The road ended abruptly in a brick wall. She reached out and touched the wall. It was a literal wall she could not get through even in her spirit form.

She released a breath, and her heart beat with excitement. The way to the Abyss was truly closed.

A single black line caught her attention. This was the only remaining thread from her previous journey. The line extended far to the east. Whatever Isabella's plan had been, even with the crack to the demon realm closed, this plan was still intact.

Valeria followed the line into the wilderness. Her magic would not let her skip forward. She traveled for hours without finding the end of the line. This was the longest she had been in the spirit realm. Even witches had an upper limit on how long they could stay here. Perhaps the goddess didn't want Valeria to see the plan yet.

Valeria returned to her body. Corona was awake, and the baby was well on the way to being born. There was still no sign of a demon.

Relief made Valeria feel like she could fly. Her ghostly body floated up in response to the feeling. She needed to return to her physical body soon.

A sonorous call echoed in the room. The urge to follow the call to its source grabbed her. Fear replaced the light feeling. If she delayed too much longer, she would follow the rest of the souls to the next place.

Valeria sank into her body just as a newborn baby squalled. No demon had come to merge with her niece.

She blinked back to the real world.

Wren had her wrapped in his arms. "What did you find?"

"The curse is gone. The crack to the demons' land is shut."

Valeria closed her eyes, knowing that the people she cared about were safe.

EPILOGUE 1: ALEX

<u>Evening, Primum seventh, 301 years post-Merge</u>

Just over a year later...

Alex closed the Archive's doors and made sure that all of the visitors were gone. He walked through the main section of the Archive, putting misplaced items back where they belong. This was important work. As soon as the words entered his head, he admitted he was lying.

Valeria should be coming soon, and he wanted to see her the moment she arrived. She was the only one who had any good information about the dragon egg. He'd searched all the records he could find and even sent off requests to find out if other archives had any data. But so far, the only thing that was known about dragons and their eggs were the few fiction books that survived from the old human world.

It had been a year, and the egg seemed no closer to hatching. Why had this happened? His gut said this was a big event.

Valeria walked up the main hall and grinned at him. "You wanted me to check the egg?"

"Yes." Alex nodded and hugged her. The year had been kind to her. The stress that had weighed her down was gone. She was now the carefree, happy woman he had caught glimpses of. When she and Wren came to the Archive to visit or to research, they fit together so well. And seemed so right for each other.

Valeria followed him to the dragon room. "Did you keep the temperature like we talked about?"

Alex nodded. "Yes, the spell you had was very useful. There are not many animals big enough to brood the egg."

Valeria nodded. "And the shell itself, has it changed?"

"I can no longer push on the outside. The shell is hard, just like we talked about."

"Good, and has the color changed?"

"No change. The egg is still big, purple, and scaled."

No matter how many times he came into this area, his chest filled with awe. This was a real, live dragon. The egg looked huge in this room. The heating spell kept the room at just the right temperature.

Valeria set her hand on the egg as she had done every week for the last year. She closed her eyes. This time, instead of her normal smile, she frowned.

His heart went to his throat. Was she detecting something wrong? Had he done something to jeopardize the egg?

"The egg is fine," Valeria said soothingly without opening her eyes. "I was just trying to get a sense of how long until the egg should hatch."

"What did you find out? " Alex put his hands in his pockets. The dust devil that followed him swirled in the hallway beyond. He took a deep breath to try and disperse the anxiety that pushed on his chest and twisted his guts.

She opened her eyes and pursed her lips. "Not too long, but there is something strange."

He raised his eyebrows.

She bit her lip and shook her head, seeming to search for words. "The dragon inside seems to be sleeping. There is something preventing the dragon from going to the next step."

"By next step, you mean hatching."

She nodded. "Yes."

"What do you sense?" What did that mean? Could the egg wait another three hundred years before hatching? Alex would give almost anything to see the baby dragon.

Valeria glanced at him quickly and then looked away. "The egg has a fate line."

"A fate line. Where have I heard that before?" Alex searched his memories but came up empty.

"I have only ever heard about it in passing." Valeria fidgeted. What could make her react in such a manner?

"What does having a fate line mean?"

"Do you remember when we did the spell to bring the Meeps together?" Valeria's next sideways look did nothing to ease his growing unease.

His magic trickled out, and the air swirled around him. He moved the magic to form another dust devil and used it to sweep the hall. There were already ten sweeping in the Archive. This was the most he'd had at once in a long time.

"Yes." That day had embedded itself in his memory as not only one of the craziest experiences of his life. He'd felt so included and special, which was weird because he was anything but special. He was just an archivist with very little magic. "You called me a protector."

His face reddened. Why did he have to say those words?

"You are." She touched his hand. "You were the reason the spell was possible."

"Me?" His voice squeaked.

Valeria laughed gently and squeezed his hand. "If you were not there, the Meeps would not have formed the egg. You were essential, and somehow that linked your fate with the fate of the dragon."

The world spun, and he found himself sitting down on the hard stone floor. "Essential? Fate?"

Valeria sat next to him. "You need to get used to the idea. In you, the dragon has part of what she needs to hatch, but there is still at least one missing piece."

"Alex!" A male voice shouted from inside the Archive. Who could be in here when it was locked up?

"Is that Max?" Valeria asked.

"Alex!" The voice got closer.

"That is Max," Valeria said tilting her head. "Interesting."

Behind them, the dragon egg cracked.

EPILOGUE 1: ISABELLA

<u>Evening, Primum seventh, 301 years post-Merge</u>

Isabella slumped against the wall of the small room she rented in the West Market. The locked door and wards would prevent anyone from scrying her location or bursting open the door.

So far, her wayward grandchild had not sought her out for direct confrontation. Grudging admiration filled Isabella's chest. She had not realized at the time that Valeria would be so strong. Isabella probably should have. No other blood relative had ever escaped a sixth-level demon's hold. Isabella had been sure that the reason Valeria had escaped was because of her cousin's sacrifice.

The passageway to the demon realm was closed. Most of her family was trapped on the other side. Only she and the three strongest demons were still in here.

Fear trickled down her spine. She was running out of time to pay the price she had agreed to with the demon lord. If she did not get the demon worlds merged, the demon lord would come for her. She swallowed the bitter taste of that thought.

She was not ready to give up her power. Many of her plans lay in ruins after the barrier snapped shut between the realms. She still had the seeds of one last plan in place, which could open the way between the worlds by destroying the natural balance.

The dryads who rallied against her powers were no match. She'd already felt her evil spreading. The darkness would soon knock on the gate of this city.

Congratulations on reaching the end of Wren and Valeria's journey! Stay tuned for a sneak peek at of the first chapter in *Shattered Oak*, the origin story of the dryad. Find out who will be knocking on the city's gate.

If you missed how Alesia and Serene met, check out **Book of Secrets**.
If you want the full story of Rose and Max, check-out **Thorn of the Rose.**

Enjoy this book? You can make a big difference...

Reviews are the most powerful tools when it comes to getting notice for my books.

If you enjoyed this book, I'd be so grateful if you'd spend just five minutes leaving a review (as short as you like)!

Thank you very much.

AUTHOR NOTES

If this is the first time you have made it to an author note, Hi!

This is where I sometimes get a little geeky about the stuff I researched to get the book together.

This book sat on my hard drive for a while, which is pretty normal for me. I had this idea of what was going to happen, but the previous book interfered! The overlap between *Thorn of the Rose* and this book had not originally been intentional. Sigh...I had to redo the timelines. Stupid writer's brain. LOL At least it was fun to take a few of the overlapping scenes and rewrite them in a new POV.

This book has Wren who is an Aero, who has feathers and has bird characteristics. Humans are all mammals and most mammals age the same way. We lose our hair or grow hair in weird places. Our hair gets gray and then white. Our skin loses its elasticity and sags.

Well, okay how do birds age? Those descendants of dinosaurs do not go gray! Feathers get their color by how they are structured. (while our hair gets its color from the chemicals compounds)

Oh, and birds do not lose feathers with age. I suppose that

makes sense or they would have a hard time flying when they get older. But how do birds get new feathers? They molt.

The last thing I was going to geek out was about the super rare ingredient for the spell to remove fire. I searched around and came up with nothing all that cool. Then I whined to a photographer friend (who also writes sci-fi and works at NASA!). She sent me the link to a picture of a bird's breath. Ah ha! That was what I needed!

Doyle, Kelly. "How to Photograph Bird Breath." North Woods Photos, December 25, 2022. https://www.northwoodsphotos. com/how-to-photograph-bird-breath/.

Eager for exclusive content? Want to be the first to know about upcoming releases and get a free short story?

Sign up for Claudia Blood's Newsletter at https://dl.bookfunnel.com/u5nf3wa84m

You can unsubscribe at any time.

SCALE OF THE DRAGON

The human world and the world of myth have merged. Ordinary individuals must become extraordinary if they hope to save it.

For 300 years, the invading evil and the natural world has balanced on a knife's edge. Something has revived the slumbering darkness and given the evil a new purpose, but the guardians are gathering...

- The dragon egg has hatched.

- The undead guardian has awoken.

- The dryad has turned warrior.

- The archivist has uncovered his long forgotten secret.

But enemies are closing in and they have an old nemesis supplying them power.

With the decay at the gates of the city, will good triumph over evil?

Find out here.

SHATTERED OAK: EXCERPT

<u>Mid-morning, Primum tenth, 100 years post-Merge</u>

Meadow Deeproot did not expect the time with her daughter to end so quickly.

"You've stayed too long." The voice was barely a whisper and was the first time anyone from the hamlet had addressed her directly. Apparently, it took being hidden in their tree for the Dryads to be brave enough to speak to a Tree Protector.

Had they always been so timid of their kin or had the war outside their protected forest finally had an impact? The world outside grew more dangerous with each passing season. The danger was the only reason she and her mate had agreed to bring their daughter to the Dryads' forest.

Doubt twisted her gut and tightened the skin in her forehead. She could still change her mind and take her daughter back home with her. But back to what? The constant fear? The battles? The uncertainty? The safe haven for the army's children had fallen and only by blind luck had Rennen not been there. Meadow took a deep breath and loosened her hands which had fisted at the thought of losing her child. This was the last safe haven, a place that would allow Rennen to discover the beauty in the world. A chance to see something stable and good. A chance for her to develop her powers without the constant fear.

"I know." Meadow nodded. Resisting the call of her mate and her duty was growing more difficult with each day. She could feel the evil upon the land and she needed to do her part to aid the good. The good needed all the help it could get. Otherwise, her mate would've come with her. But instead, he'd said his farewells from his commander's tent. The huskiness of his voice and the slight tremor of his hands had given away his feelings. The memory of him in pain closed her throat and reminded her of what was to come. She too would need to give her goodbyes. "I need to say goodbye."

Her stomach twisted. She was not ready to let go, but she must. Rennen must stay at the Hamlet because of the cursed boy born on the same day. Her gaze swept to the edge of the play area where the pale, dark-haired boy stood. Gant shuffled his feet like he wanted to run and hide, but his gaze was fixed on Rennen. She filled a bucket from the stream, oblivious to the unease around her.

"She must stay." The invisible speaker reminded Meadow.

A wisp of anger trickled into Meadow's body leaving her very aware of how different she was from the rest of the hamlet's docile citizens. To maintain balance, the Earth Mother had made Tree Protectors more passionate and more motivated to action because their main purpose was to rid the world of cursed Dryads. What better tool could the Earth Mother have chosen than a 'good' Dryad to fight a 'bad' Dryad? But nothing was ever that simple. Good and bad were just a series of choices and actions. And this moment was a pivotal choice for her daughter's future.

A squeal drew Meadow's attention back to her daughter. Rennen still held the bucket but now she stood behind a sopping wet little girl who darted into her tree. The other green-haired children slipped away, leaving Rennen alone. She would get used to being alone. Deep conflicted feelings twisted in Meadow's chest at the thought of Rennen experiencing the same loneliness Meadow had here. Loneliness was better than fear. Better than learning so young how fragile life was.

"B-but she said she needed to be watered." Rennen's words came out in a wail.

Meadow covered her mouth to keep from laughing and leaned closer to her old tree. No tree behind the veil that protected the hamlet would house a Dryad that embraced her fate and transformed fully into a Tree Protector. Still, she placed her head against the tree and hoped the tree might remember her.

The tree was silent. A tree outside the veil might allow her to stay for a night or more, but the tree would never be her home. She'd given up so much for what she believed in. And she would give up more. The sorrow ached with each breath, adding to the feeling of finality. She would have to leave her daughter today and go back to her mate.

"She is just like you were." The voice sounded faintly exasperated.

"Yes, she is." That loosened something in Meadow's chest. Growing up in the Hamlet would not be easy on Rennen, but she would survive. They would not understand her extra energy, drive to help, or how deeply she would feel. It wouldn't be long before they started to avoid Rennen. At least she would have a friend. Even if he was cursed, he should ease some of her loneliness.

"You were only trying to help." Gant was at Rennen's side and laid a hand on her shoulder.

"I was trying to save her." She sounded so confused and mournful. Meadow could not see her face but could imagine her lower lip sticking out and the pouty frown.

Gant wrapped Rennen in a hug. She wriggled out a moment later and scampered away into the underbrush. He followed after her.

"Could she be the one to lift the curse and merge the lines?" The voice sounded so hopeful.

But Meadow knew already, Rennen was not the chosen one. That spark between Rennen and Gant had gone only one direction. If the fates had been kind, the two would have had an instant bonding and given the good its first victory. If they'd had that victory, it might have been all the world needed to push back the invaders. If they could have defied the invaders, she might have been able to raise her daughter in peace with her mate.

But none of that was to be. She rubbed at the ache in her chest. If she told the truth, she could keep her daughter and bring her back to the front-lines of a losing war. If she hedged, Rennen would stay here and be far safer, but she would be without her family and would be barely understood or tolerated. Meadow's head ached at the no-win choice before her.

"Maybe." Meadow's chest felt as if it was cracking open. Hopefully, she'd made the right choice for her daughter and her future safety and happiness.

Find out what happened to Rennen.

ACKNOWLEDGMENTS

Thanks to my hubby and family who allow me to wander away when I need to write.

To my VA Kelly I can't thank you enough for your undying enthusiasm and design sense. Social media is way less scary with you on my side.

To my amazing developmental editor Dawn Alexander who helped me organize my chaos and keep my inner achiever from getting too enthusiastic.

Thank you Fenley Grant for your amazing editing skills and for working me in when I am inevitably late.

Thank you Wendy for reading and giving feedback to my writing since college. (A scary number of years ago) You were always able to find a nugget of good that kept me going.

Thank you to the ladies at Lakehouse Writers group, Tammy, Val, MaryAnna, B, Jay, and Kim who have been a constant source of inspiration, motivation, and sanity checking.

Thank you to Val and MaryAnna who kept me honest on our accountability texts and for helping me figure out the end of this book. You both were so patient with my what-if-ing.

Thank you Antha and Christine for the many, many, many writing sprints. Without you guys I never would have gotten the book done.

Thank you to Calley for the daily checkins. Cookies!

ABOUT THE AUTHOR

Claudia Blood writes mystical realms and futuristic worlds, where underdogs defy authority, defeat demons, and discover their destined family amidst the chaos.

Her love of urban Fantasies led her from life as a research scientist right into that of an award-winning author. With works such as the Renegades Rising, *Relic trilogy*, <u>*Merged* series</u>, and the <u>Supernatural Detective Agency</u>. Claudia Blood's works cover a wide range of genres and themes that have captivated many.

For her latest release, visit her at
<u>www.ClaudiaBlood.com</u>